The Gangster's Wife by A

# The Gangster's Wife by Anne Brooke

## Chapter One

Elise Walker wasn't an emotional woman. She had always prided herself on the coldness of her heart, if she admitted to possessing such an artefact. However, even she had to admit to a certain frisson of horror when she entered her home after an ordinary day at the office to find her husband stretched out on the hall floor, his hand clutched to his throat and most definitely, in her non-medical opinion, dead.

"Oh, Gerald," she said, her own hand clutching her throat in a strange echo of his gesture. "What on earth have you done?"

Her first instinctive words weren't particularly accusatory concerning her unfortunate husband's predicament, but in all honesty Elise couldn't think what else to say. Then again, words would do no good when Gerald had moved beyond her reach to meet his Maker in the ultimate story. Besides, Elise had several important decisions to make.

One of these decisions was not to waste time on further words at all. Instead, Elise dredged deep in her folk memory to see if she had any first aid skills left from her younger, more caring years. Astonishingly, she found some and spent the next few moments listening to see if Gerald was still breathing (no sign of it), searching for a heartbeat (ditto) and then, for lack of any other knowledge, placing him as best she could into the recovery position. Or rather, what she remembered of it, but she did admit she might have failed in terms of exactly where to put his arms.

Finally, she managed this not entirely necessary task, and then and only then did she step round his inert form and reach for the telephone in the hallway.

"Hello," she said, surprised to hear how steady her own voice was at this challenging time. "Ambulance, please."

It took ten minutes to arrive, which, bearing in mind the amount of roadworks through Elise's home village in the leafy county of Surrey, was much to be admired. They must have driven like the wind or been lurking in the vicinity waiting for disasters.

In the time between discovering Gerald and the arrival of the emergency medical team, for what good it would do anyone, Elise sat next to her dead husband and leant against the wall. The radiator was reassuringly warm against her back. She put her hand on his cooling forehead and thought about their life together.

Their relationship hadn't begun as a passionate affair, not by any measure, but in the beginning it had seemed like a good idea and over the years it had worked its way into their lives and turned out to be something rather important. Perhaps even special. Elise didn't feel a *great* loss, necessarily, but it was certainly a meaningful one. This wasn't because either of them had fallen into an extramarital affair which had gone terribly sour and they'd turned to each other for comfort and support in the aftermath. This scenario had always made them laugh. Really, it was beyond ridiculous.

In fact, neither Elise nor Gerald were keen fans of any other serious relationship apart from the one they had with each other. The only other verging-on-serious relationship Elise had experienced before she met Gerald had been with a student of theology at the university where she herself had studied English. She'd liked the man as a friend, but it had never gone any deeper for her, though he – his name had been Nigel, she remembered suddenly – had been keen on her for some reason and had been very upset when she'd ended it as politely as possible after six months had passed. In all honesty, she'd been getting a little bored with his intentions and the one time he'd kissed her with considerable passion, she'd not enjoyed it much. Though, of course, she'd never said so. That would have been impolite, and Elise prided herself on her courtesy.

Gerald too held great store by courtesy. When they'd first met, in London, he'd made sure he walked on the outer side of the pavement as they were making their way to the tube station together in order to protect her from the cars. Elise at the time had thought she didn't need protecting from anything, let alone a mere car, but had appreciated the gesture. They'd both been in their early twenties and had been married just a year later. No passion, not then at any rate, just affection and reason. Passion had come later. Thankfully, the affection and reason had remained, and had worked very well for the next thirty years of their married life, except now Gerald had ended it.

Damn him, he was just fifty-five years old. Too young to die of anything as clichéd as a heart attack. And, at a mere fifty-three years old, Elise was far too young to be a widow. It wasn't an option she would have chosen.

A wave of sudden tears powered over her and she therefore wasn't prepared at all when the doorbell rang. She struggled to her feet and wiped one hand over her eyes as she opened the inner door. The ambulance blocked the driveway. She hadn't even been aware of a siren. Had they had it on, or had she been so lost in her thoughts that she'd not concentrated on how Gerald needed her to perform these last few duties?

When she opened the door, Elise tried to speak, to explain what had happened, but, strangely, she couldn't make her voice work. It didn't matter. The two ambulance men took control and the next Elise knew, she was sitting in the dining room with a cup of tea she couldn't drink – provided by the taller of the two men – whilst the other did whatever needed to be done to Gerald. Elise didn't like to think about it so she concentrated on the garden instead. Gerald had always loved the garden. He wouldn't want her to neglect it, though frankly there was not much she could do about nature in winter. Early December wasn't conducive to gardening. Five minutes or so after that, one of their local doctors arrived. The ambulance men must have called her. Elise couldn't remember the last time either Gerald or she had gone to the surgery. Perhaps, bearing in mind what had happened today, they should have gone more often. Heavens, she must stop thinking this way, especially as she felt an overwhelming urge to laugh and that wouldn't do at all.

Not having a close relationship with her local doctor didn't matter, as it was obvious Elise wasn't required to act in a hospitable manner or make any key decisions. All she had to do was sip her tea, nod every now and again, and accept sympathy, both spoken and unspoken. There was nothing useful she could do, as Gerald was dead. Nothing anyone did would bring her husband back to life again, so she felt quite content – if this was the word she sought – letting the professionals do whatever they needed to do.

After a while, Elise noticed another woman who wasn't the doctor had arrived and was busy smoothing things over and making yet more tea. Elise wasn't sure she needed more tea. She didn't think it was doing her any good. She wondered briefly about asking if Gerald should have a cup if its reviving qualities were so profound, but thought if she said so, then she might never be rid of the medical profession at her door.

The presence of the woman she was unable to place puzzled her. Elise felt it was someone she ought to know, or know of, but she couldn't quite remember her name or where she came from. She was pleasant enough, however: a short, fair-haired woman who exuded confidence and compassion in equal measures. It was only when the doctor said her name, "Lottie", that Elise managed to work out the woman's identity.

It was her neighbour from two doors away. Of course it was. How could she forget such a thing? Still, neither Elise nor Gerald were the sociable types, and constantly lived with the light embarrassment of a forgotten name or three. They preferred a life of quiet withdrawal to the hurly-burly of the world outside.

However, Lottie often held neighbourly get-togethers, and Elise and Gerald had always gone along, though they tended to remain on the outskirts. These events were surprisingly good but Elise was neither skilled nor interested in small-talk. Chat wasn't her greatest talent.

For the remainder of the evening – Gerald's last on this earth and in their home – Elise simply let things happen as they would. At one point, she found herself in the local hospital, with Lottie at her side, and agreeing with whatever the officials there wanted to do with Gerald's body. Words drifted past her, only some of them reaching what must have been their mark. At another stage in this long, stretched-out evening, Elise became aware she was holding Lottie's hand so tightly she wondered if she'd ever be able to let go. And what would happen when she did.

Finally, at the end of the night, Elise arrived back at her own front door, Lottie still at her side like a friendly, all-seeing shadow. If shadows could even see, or would want to. Elise was so tired that she could have abandoned any ambition of going to bed on this, the first night of her widowhood, and simply stretched out across her threshold and let the elements and people rage around her in whichever way they felt appropriate.

Such behaviour would of course be most unacceptable in Surrey and she was sure it wouldn't be tolerated, more from kindness than disgust. In any case, Lottie, bless her, would never have countenanced it. She was too socially concerned a woman: it was a gift Elise had never possessed but which she was grateful for now.

The other reason she would not have been permitted to lie like a tramp or a guard dog across the front door was the presence of the police officers. When Lottie had parked the car across the front of Elise's drive, Elise had been only vaguely aware of the lurking shape of the police car waiting on the other side of the road. She'd even admonished herself for assuming it was anything to do with herself. Just because her husband – poor Gerald! – had died today, it didn't mean she was the centre of the local universe. Lives went on elsewhere, and why on earth shouldn't they? Before entering her home once more, Elise even watched and wondered if there might be about to be some mistake as the two police officers got out of the car and began to stroll, almost casually, in her direction.

Lottie waited, silent but companionable, at her side.

"Mrs. Walker?" the nearest of the two police officers spoke as he stepped onto her drive. "May we have a word?"

He was a tall man, towering over his smaller, female colleague, who looked very young indeed. Almost too young to have such a responsible job. Elise wondered if this might be the poor woman's first assignment and if she'd been chosen simply because she was female. Some things never changed, no matter how many years went by.

"Can it wait till morning?" Lottie spoke first and her hand was warm and steadying on Elise's arm. "It's been a terrible evening. I think Mrs. Walker needs to rest."

"No, it's fine," Elise cut in, and gave Lottie's hand a gentle squeeze. "Whatever it is, I'd rather do it now. I mean, what else can happen to make things any worse than they already are? I'd much rather put all my sorrows into one day, if I can."

The younger, female officer glanced away and seemed to swallow, while the elder one coughed.

"Well, Mrs. Walker," he said and this time his voice was far more hesitant. "It's about your husband. If it's not too difficult for you, we do need to talk to you about Mr. Gerald Walker, and the sooner the better."

# Chapter Two

There was never any arguing with the police, Elise decided as she made coffee for her two visitors. Lottie had gone home, even though she'd offered to stay. But the expression on the faces of the two officers made Elise's decision for her. They looked like people who needed to say something only she should hear.

Elise had assumed the day couldn't get any worse, but she had no guarantee. With Gerald's death, she was truly alone. Damn the man, but she could have done with his presence now. As she poured the coffee, she paused to allow the expected wave of grief to wash over her, as it had done earlier.

It didn't. Instead, Elise felt only a strange sense of excitement as if a very peculiar adventure was about to begin. One she might even like, though of course she would have preferred to have any chosen adventures with her husband. They were a team, or had been.

Might she do all right on her own? Heavens, it was too early to say, far too early. It would be appalling to dance on Gerald's grave before it was even dug, however tentative her steps. All these deliberations were something Elise could most definitely not show to the police, so she composed her face before she took their refreshments through on a tray. It was the shock, undoubtedly, she told herself.

In the living room, the officers were sitting on the cream leather sofa, the woman on the left, and the man on the right. Elise felt a flash of pure fury whip through her. The right-hand position on the sofa was Gerald's place and this man had no business to be sitting on it. The female officer sat in Elise's usual position, but she had no energy to be concerned about such a thing. It was Gerald she was worried about, and he was dead so the whole reaction was deeply ridiculous and far too emotional. Not a state Elise enjoyed at any level.

She needed to keep calm. And she wasn't going to be made to wait to find out whatever they were here for either.

"There you are," she said, as she placed the requested drinks in front of each of her guests. "One coffee, white with no sugar. And one black with two sugars. Though I would draw the dangers of sugar to your attention. You won't get away with it once you get older, I can tell you. Anyway, whatever you need to ask me, I'd be pleased if you would do it now. Thank you."

There, Elise thought. She sounded confident enough, didn't she? Though perhaps not quite as in mourning as she should be. Nonetheless, she didn't want to appear to be a woman who could be trifled with, as she most certainly wasn't such a woman, and never would be. She sat, sipped at her glass of water, gazed at the officers and waited.

To her surprise, it was the female officer who responded. Elise had assumed she was the token woman there to mop up any tears, but was happy to find out she'd been wrong. Maybe the dreaded glass ceiling wasn't too tough after all. She hoped not. In the meantime, the officer was speaking.

"Thank you, Mrs. Walker," she said. "We're very grateful for your forbearance and for being willing to see us today. We're very sorry for your loss. I'm Constable Cooper and my colleague here is Sergeant Bradley. We've been assigned to your case, or rather your husband's, for a while."

She looked as if she were intending to say more, but Elise's curiosity was well and truly piqued. "My husband's case? He's not been murdered. He died of natural causes, a heart attack, according to our doctor."

Constable Cooper nodded. "Yes, we've no dispute there. What I mean is that we've been working on your husband's case for a while, and there are a number of missing pieces of information we believe you can help us with, if you're willing to."

Elise blinked. She wondered for a moment if this might be some kind of dreadful joke and even now Gerald was about to come bursting into her room and back into her life, yelling "surprise!" But no, neither her husband nor she had ever put much faith in surprises. They weren't that sort of couple.

"I have to say," Elise replied, fixing both officers with a very searching stare. "I have absolutely no idea what you're talking about so perhaps you'd better start from the beginning. The *very* beginning."

And they did.

According to them, Gerald had been a criminal. Not the kind of criminal who killed people or caused any injuries, Elise was happy to hear. No, Gerald didn't like violence and would do almost anything to avoid it. This Elise could vouch for; her husband had disliked any kind of confrontation with a vengeance. In their early married days, Elise had once had to coax poor Gerald out of the spare room with the promise of chocolates and sex in order to speed recovery from what *he'd* called a row and what *she'd* understood to be simply a way of telling him about her very difficult working day. She'd learnt several things that evening, not all of which were a matter for public record, though she remembered it as having in the end been very enjoyable. One of the most practical things she'd learnt had been that when Elise raised her voice to express her opinions about what mattered to her, even though it had nothing to do with her husband, Gerald interpreted this as shouting at him personally and tried to avoid it at all costs. It had been a curious conundrum which Elise had – after a good few years, it had to be said – solved by the simple addition of a statement at the start of her emoting telling Gerald it was nothing to do with him, but she was just cross. A few years later, he'd even learnt it was all right to hug her when she was upset and shouting, and this made things a lot better very quickly.

However, he'd always been a clever kind of man, if not an overtly emotional one. Far cleverer than she herself would ever be, a fact which had in the beginning irked her, but which she'd grown used to, and indeed had come to rely on. He lived almost entirely in the brain, except of course at those times when it mattered that he didn't.

She'd never thought of him as anything but a model citizen. Now, listening to the police officers' brief resume of Gerald's criminal career, she found herself feeling rather impressed. She hoped it was true.

"You mean," she said, interrupting the flow. "You mean you believe my husband was a white-collar criminal who stole thousands of pounds from big business and never got caught? Is this what you're telling me?"

"Yes, that's exactly it," Sergeant Bradley confirmed with a brief nod. He'd taken over the narrative some time ago from his underling. "We've had our eye on him for years and tried to get proof but were never able to. He was always at least one step ahead of us. Now he's dead, we'd like to search his computers to see if we can discover anything more about what's been going on. I do know it might be too soon to raise the issue, but Mr. Walker's network was very slick and will even now be cutting its losses and making sure their activities are as hidden as possible. We need to act fast and we'd like you to help us, if we're going to have a greater chance of recovering the stolen monies."

The sergeant paused and looked at Elise as if the matter of her agreement was a simple one. He looked like a man who expected a yes. Elise, on the other hand, wasn't anywhere near that stage, and didn't like being rushed into decisions at the best of times, no matter who was doing the rushing.

So she gazed coolly back. "That's all very well, but I'm going to need a lot more information, and certainly a lot more proof."

One hour later, the police had departed and Elise was ready for bed. She'd only managed to get rid of the two officers by promising to visit them for what they described as a *further briefing* the next day. Thankfully tomorrow was a Friday so she didn't need to worry about work. Though then again, she supposed her sudden widowhood meant work could be safely set to one side for a while. She hadn't needed to work on a Friday as Gerald earned a good enough salary to ensure she didn't have to work full-time.

Heavens, was his high salary a sign of his illicit dealings, and the building company he worked for hadn't been doing so well after all? Elise almost spat her toothpaste into the sink as the possibility gripped her. If the police were right, was she living on immoral earnings? If they were right, she'd have to sell the house and find something on her own, wouldn't she?

The thought made her feel quite queasy. Elise and Gerald had pushed the proverbial boat out rather beyond their means (or what she imagined their means had been) ten years ago when they'd bought this house, and she'd always loved it. They'd lived most of their marriage up to that point in an old Victorian house, so the joys of a modern home in the countryside, with large windows and views across fields had been a revelation. The light at both morning and evening always made Elise's heart sing, if she was the kind of woman whose heart was prone to singing.

She didn't think she was, and most definitely not today when she'd just been widowed. But nonetheless her house was her domain and she was reluctant to leave it, whether or not it had been the result of criminal earnings. If the police were right – and this was still be to proven – then they'd have a good battle on their hands if they thought Elise would give anything back which they thought she shouldn't have.

Gerald might have been wilier than the authorities, but she too was a force to be reckoned with. Gerald had always said so, in those rare times when he offered a few words without being prompted. He'd not been much of a man for words. Perhaps he'd been too busy doing wrong to have time for it.

Once more on this sadly notable day, Elise swallowed down a rising hysteria and rinsed her mouth from the remains of the toothpaste. She obviously wasn't very good at being a widow, but then again it wasn't the kind of situation they wrote about much in books. Perhaps they should.

Earlier on, after persuading her to attend the station on Friday, the police had asked if there was anyone they could call to come and be with her for the night.

The thought sent shudders down Elise's spine. She'd already persuaded Lottie to go back home, and she was in no fit state to cope with anyone else. She had to be strong to deal with people around her, and today wasn't a day for strength.

If she tried to explain her position on company to the police, she couldn't see them even beginning to understand so instead she'd lied with great aplomb and told them she was staying at Lottie's for the night. They appeared to believe her, thank goodness, and had left shortly after.

Unfortunately after the police had departed, Lottie had rung. She must have been on the look out and keen to offer support. Either that, or keen to find out what on earth was going on. Elise couldn't blame her as she thought she would have felt exactly the same. Lottie very kindly offered to stay the night with Elise or to put up a bed for her at her own house.

Despite her natural inclinations, Elise was sorely tempted to follow either of those options, but she was not the kind of woman to put off whatever tasks she was honour bound to face today. One of these self-allotted tasks was to sleep in the house for the first time on her own. She could no longer rely on Gerald. Neither did she feel able to cope with wearing a front for interaction with any more people; she'd had enough of the kindness of strangers.

So Elise had refused Lottie's offer and was alone, in truth, at last.

Her routine was almost the same as every night, in fact. In her marriage, it had been Elise's task to make sure all the doors were locked and the windows tight shut. Tonight, she'd already locked up downstairs and turned off the hall light. The only light in the house now came from her bedroom and the upstairs landing. As usual, she'd washed her face and brushed her teeth in the main bathroom on the old side of the house – though not that old as it had only been built in the 1960s. The ensuite in the bedroom had been Gerald's domain.

Foolish woman. She could easily have used it tonight, but no, she couldn't quite bring herself to do such a thing. Not so soon. She might find no issue at all in sleeping in the house by herself on the night her husband had died, but his essence was still present. She couldn't bear to use 'his' bathroom. Such an act was beyond her.

Slowly Elise made sure the internal doors on the old side of the house were all shut. It wasn't strictly necessary but she'd been advised to shut doors before going to sleep by a fire officer a long time ago, and she'd always remembered it. Gerald had never understood her compulsion, but he'd accepted it – this was how their marriage had worked.

She would need to make her widowhood work too. Tonight, however, she had simply to endure it. Tomorrow and the days after, she would find a way to live, for herself. So, without thinking too deeply, Elise crossed the landing and gently closed the door of Gerald's study before retiring to bed.

Sleep, of course, was another matter.

Gerald might have died but, understandably perhaps, he hadn't yet entirely left. His pillow still bore the slight indentation where his head had lain on it the night before, his last night on the earth and the last time he would ever sleep here. Almost of its own accord, Elise's hand stretched out across the sheets – she always slept on the right side of the bed and neither of them would ever have countenanced a duvet – and found his pyjamas. Neatly folded as always and placed with a military precision under the top of his two pillows, in the exact centre. Gerald was a man who enjoyed the comfort of order, a character trait which had suited Elise perfectly.

He would never need his pyjamas again. Elise supposed she would have to put them in the laundry and then give them to a charity shop, but it wasn't a task she could face in the immediate future. And perhaps not for a while, in spite of all her reason.

So she gave the brushed navy cotton pyjamas (with slight stripe) a gentle pat and left them exactly where they were. Gerald, she imagined, would have appreciated her delicacy. At least, the man she had thought she knew would have. The other Gerald – the one with the possible criminal past – was more unknowable.

Tonight wasn't a time for this new and perhaps more exciting Gerald, however. The new Gerald, if such a man could exist after death, would be confronted tomorrow. Elise needed, at least for as long as she was able to, to remember the husband she'd known.

## Chapter Three

When she had met Gerald, Elise had been at her most vulnerable, with both parents dead. She had been desperate for connection with the outside world away from the pain of memory, and in Gerald she had found her answer. He had always been protective of her and she'd thought he was at heart one of life's gentlemen.

She wondered for the first time if the role she'd allocated to him had been as much a burden for him then as it had become for her, now. She had no way of knowing. Odd how she'd always thought she'd be the first one to die. In dying before her, Gerald had taken her by surprise.

Though Elise had never been exactly in love with Gerald, she had grown to love him and to trust him over the years. She missed his silent presence next to her on the sofa. One of the most intimate things they had ever done together was to read. Sex had in the end been very good indeed, but reading, ah reading was what had united them in a way nothing else could.

Elise picked up her book from her bedside table and for the first time started to read alone. Tonight she was continuing on from the first few chapters of a book she'd heard described as a literary comedy of manners, Laurie Graham's *At Sea*. So far she was enjoying it, though she could tell the husband was likely to prove difficult. Elise tended to distrust people who went on cruises, even though she and Gerald had both enjoyed and endured a river cruise once, on the Nile, many years ago.

As a couple, they preferred to do their own exploring, at a time of their own choosing, and being part of a cruise had meant they were at the beck and call, every moment of the day, of the itinerary. This had been fine for the first one or two days as the joy of being lazy had proved alluring. But when one was rushed between different museums and temples at a pace which could only kindly be described as brisk, the novelty had soon worn off. Elise and Gerald preferred to take their own time in finding out about a town and its culture, but the choice of opting out had not been a possibility and would, in any case, probably have been frowned upon. Cruise travellers did activities together, not alone.

Halfway through the trip, Gerald and Elise had however managed to sneak away for an hour or so whilst exploring Abu Simbel. Whilst the rest of the coach-load discovered the history of the Aswan dam, Elise and Gerald simply sat in front of the great temple and gazed. For a while they even held hands, no words necessary, in a way they had never done, not even when their courtship began.

Elise had, for once in her life, found herself in tears as she tried to take in the great artefact. She couldn't have explained why, not fully. It was something to do with the fact that, as a young girl growing up in the countryside, her father had given her a book on Egypt and the section about Abu Simbel had been her favourite. She had read it over and over again, and her father had remarked how pleased he was that his daughter was so immersed in history. The subject of the past had been her father's special delight, although most of the time, he had preferred matters of war, which Elise had not.

It was something to do then with the fact Elise had always longed to visit the temple of her childhood memory, but had never hoped to get to Egypt. She hated flying quite such a long way, and until now her only trips had been to Europe.

Now, even if the cruise had been too regimented, she would be forever grateful she'd had the opportunity to see this mystical place. She knew then and there she would never see it again. What astonished her most was the unexpected mixture of the old and the new. The temple itself was entirely intact but in recent years it had been moved further up the hill while the Aswan dam was recreated in all its current glory. Elise had wondered if the magic of having the midsummer's day morning sun shine through the caverns until it reached the innermost part of the temple itself would have been lost. She was delighted to discover it had not, and this strange miraculous blending of the old and the new had left a particular brand on her heart.

It reminded her of Gerald and how they were. They had been old and new together, in their ways, and Elise didn't know if she could find a way to simply be new, on her own.

However, it was stupid to get upset by what she couldn't change. Gerald was gone. She would have to make a new life on her own, and in a way which best suited her.

Elise brought the reading light closer and read her book. She could escape from her mind and her life most effectively in the pages of a book. One day, as work colleagues occasionally nagged her, she might even get a Kindle, but real touchable pages were her preferred drug of choice. The only drug she'd ever had. She sighed and settled in for a night in her own company.

# Chapter Four

In the morning, her new life and all its challenges remained.

Elise hadn't been expecting any kind of police attention. Heavens, she'd not been expecting a dead husband yesterday either. It was not proving a good week for her. Nonetheless, she had no choice but to get into her car and drive to the police station to try to find out more about what was going on. Or rather, what the local constabulary thought was going on.

As she closed the front door behind her, the December clouds filled the skies and she could smell rain in the air. A sharp frost had patterned the car windows with an almost impenetrable layer, and Gerald's car was in the way so she couldn't move her own without moving his.

Odd how it felt like the most frustrating event since the discovery of his body in the hallway. She'd never enjoyed driving his 4x4 when Gerald was alive, so the chances of her benefiting from the experience now were extremely low. Damn the man, couldn't he have parked the car on the road before coming indoors and having his heart attack? No, she supposed in all honesty he couldn't. She liked to think of herself as a reasonable and compassionate woman.

With a sigh, Elise retraced her steps and searched for Gerald's car key in its usual place in the key basket on the hall cupboard. It wasn't there. Well, it had to be somewhere as he'd driven home and parked it, hadn't he? Sometimes, if he was careless, it fell behind the cupboard and became trapped against the wall. Only last year, the two of them had spent ages searching for it one hectic morning, and of course it had been the last place they'd looked.

Elise shook her head. Gerald would never now be in anything resembling a rush again. Did that mean she would have to rush for the both of them? It was hard to say and too complicated to consider.

This time, taking the easiest option first, she hunkered down and pulled the nearest end of the cupboard towards her. The chink of metal on the wooden floor told of her success, and she grabbed the keys. Oh how these small successes could be so immensely satisfying. She'd saved all that time searching fruitlessly elsewhere, and a thrill of achievement flowed through her. This was her first *After Gerald* victory and, though small, she would milk it for all it was worth. After all, there was nobody here to tell her otherwise.

As Elise, still triumphant, stood up, a flash of white on the floor near where the keys had lain drew her eye. It was a small scrap of paper. She hated mess, so she picked it up and folded it open. One word was scrawled across it in Gerald's handwriting and looked as if it had been written in a hurry: *Allotment*.

Elise blinked. How odd. Their village had an area for allotments, of course. Had Gerald been wanting to have one of them at some point? He'd never discussed it with her, that was for sure. How very curious. Still, she wouldn't be any kind of a good widow if she threw her husband's possible last note away, so she folded it back up and placed it in her handbag. Then she left and carried on with the task of moving Gerald's car without taking most of the neighbour's trees and front lawn flowers – not to mention her own – with it. Honestly, the beast was a veritable tank. She much preferred her own very zippy

Fiesta. She had never known why Gerald needed such a mode of transport. It was not that he'd needed to compensate for any physical lack elsewhere – as it were – and he certainly wasn't an offroader fan. Utterly the opposite.

Lots of things in life were a mystery and possibly one she would never solve. So she decided to put this particular one, like many things in her life, to one side, and do whatever came to hand. An admirable philosophy.

The journey to the police station took fifteen minutes and Elise managed to avoid the potholes on the way, mainly as she knew most of them already. The Surrey village where she and Gerald had made their home didn't have a station, perhaps because until now crime hadn't been a major issue. Elise wondered if it should have been, if what the police believed about her husband proved true. However, the small town nearby was apparently a crime magnet, and the police station had pride of place in the High Street.

Elise parked in Waitrose car park and made her way across the road to the police station. She ignored the notices in the car park telling her not to park there unless she actually wanted to do any shopping, just as all the locals did. Only the summer tourists obeyed such nonsense.

Once in the police station, which she'd never before had cause to visit, Elise's first thought was how dull the foyer was. They could at least have made it more amenable for the casual passerby to come in and report crimes. Instead, the shabby grey walls and torn posters were more than enough to put off any concerned citizen. If she'd come here to report a crime, she might well have been put off at the first hurdle and gone back to Waitrose for a latte instead. The prices there were crime enough. How very *Surrey* she was – Gerald had been right about her. And, really, there was nothing wrong with it either. He'd said it with laughter, she recalled.

A fresh-faced and ridiculously young policeman stood behind the reception desk. When Elise made her business known, he nodded and invited her to take a seat while he trotted backstage to advise his superiors. She smiled politely but didn't take him up on his offer. No doubt there'd be plenty of sitting down very soon.

After a while, Constable Cooper appeared, and Elise prepared herself for whatever revelations were to come.

"Please, come through to our interview room," she said. "Would you like a coffee?"

Elise declined. She couldn't imagine the coffee here would be good quality. She would live without. The interview room kept up with the traditions of the station foyer, but thankfully without the shabby posters. She could cope with the excessive grey, almost.

Sergeant Bradley was already seated, with a foul-smelling liquid in a cup and a file of papers at his side. He was staring with a frown at a laptop. Elise sat opposite him while Constable Cooper spread out the papers from her file on the table. As far as Elise could see, these were a series of bank statements from an account whose number she didn't recognise. She recognised the name attached to it, however. It was Gerald's.

"These are my husband's accounts?" she asked, just to make sure she wasn't missing something entirely obvious.

"Yes," confirmed Sergeant Bradley, who hadn't even welcomed her here. Common courtesies obviously weren't his forte. "Mr. Walker set up this account about two years ago. He's had a series of others in the past, of course, over the last ten to fifteen years. But he's been subtle enough to change them whenever he thought we were getting too close. Though, as with this one, he did reuse several of them later. It's taken us a great deal of effort to keep up with him."

"But you never managed to catch him actually doing anything illegal, did you?" Elise cut in, suddenly feeling inordinately proud of her secretive criminal husband. "Or surely you would have said something to him before this."

Sergeant Bradley turned red, and white, and then red again, while the constable studied her fingernails with grave concentration. Elise had obviously hit on a nerve, but she couldn't find it in herself to feel sorry for upsetting the law. For the first time she could remember, she wondered if she were not necessarily on the side of the good people. This felt surprisingly liberating. She followed up her advantage.

"So, if any of what you're about to tell me is true, then whatever he might have been, my husband was in fact cleverer than you, and for rather a long time. He was also more polite, as you've not even welcomed me or thanked me for coming here yet."

Sergeant Bradley cleared his throat and blinked, while the constable made a sound that might have been a laugh. Elise didn't bother to ascertain whether it was or not. She simply continued to gaze steadily at the sergeant.

"I'm sorry," he said in the end, but Elise thought the sorrow couldn't have been truly heartfelt. "We do appreciate your attending the station, especially so early on in your mourning period."

Goodness. Elise couldn't help being impressed by such terminology. She was sure the phrase 'mourning period' hadn't been used since Queen Victoria was on the throne, but she'd always approved of resurrecting old phrases. Tradition should be more respected than it, sadly, was.

"Thank you," she said, knowing courtesy should be responded to only with courtesy, no matter how late its arrival. "So why don't you tell me what you know, and we'll see how we go from there. But, in all honesty, I'm going to need convincing."

Over the next hour and a half, the combined might of Officers Bradley and Cooper – which began to sound more and more like a firm of solicitors as the conversation continued – slowly convinced Elise that at the very least they believed wholeheartedly in their case. And, heavens above, it might actually be true.

She couldn't help being impressed, both by Gerald's subtle cunning and the sheer determination of the police. Somehow it felt rather reassuring to live in a country which gave rise, on the one hand, to people who could use their intelligence so very cleverly in making money, and, on the other hand, also provided bloody-minded officers of the law to bring them to justice.

At every stage of whatever operations Gerald had been involved in, he'd always – always – been one step ahead. Good for him, Elise found herself thinking and then had to subdue the thought. She didn't want it to show too much on her face when in the company of the police. She didn't want to get herself arrested, after all.

The money Gerald had made had been accomplished through illicit activities which were mainly in the realms of illegal art exports, with the odd antiquity thrown in.

Antiquities were – apparently – harder to conceal than the usual brand of artworks. Elise supposed that those handling the goods could more easily roll up a canvas than they could an object made from iron or wood. At least, it was what she assumed though the police didn't specify. And she didn't want to ask too many idiotic questions. She could imagine very well how very stupid she must seem to them not to have known any of this about her dead husband, and she didn't want to justify their initial impressions.

Then again, if Gerald, in his obviously deeply ingrained criminality, had managed to fool the police all these years, then it wouldn't be too much of a leap of skill to fool her too. And he had, hadn't he? On the other hand, perhaps she'd not been paying him enough attention when he'd been trying to tell her in his subtle husbandly way all the time? A shocking concept indeed.

No, that couldn't be true, in any measure. Gerald wasn't a communicative man by nature and she could well believe he'd kept many secrets from her, including this one. He wasn't a disloyal husband – or she hoped he'd not been – but he preferred to plough his own furrow without reference to his wife.

It was how she preferred it also.

Finally, the police told her that in the last few days, when they'd been really close to beating Gerald at his own game – as they put it to her, though she didn't entirely believe them – he'd taken all the money they'd been tracking out of his usual online accounts and put it somewhere they couldn't trace. All one hundred thousand pounds of it. Good for him was her first response! She wondered where it was now. Nonetheless, there were other aspects of these revelations from the constabulary she needed to know more about. How they affected her, for one.

By now, the two officers were peering over Elise's shoulder, both of them still rapt with the excitement of their explanations. They almost seemed to have forgotten her presence entirely in their eagerness to explore all avenues of Gerald's criminal activities. Elise wondered for a moment about the modern world where virtual crime such as this could result in such evident glee. In the lines of the old phrase, weren't there real-life villains to catch out there? It was perhaps easier to indulge in detection by computer rather than running after criminals caught in the act. Time to bring them back to real life. *Her* real life.

"That's all very well and good," Elise said, stopping both officers in the flow of something or other. She hadn't been paying attention during the last few moments. "That's all very well, but there are one or two additional facts I'd like to know. Why are you telling me all this instead of questioning me if you think I might be involved? I'm Gerald's widow. What's to say I might not know something about what you're telling me? The second and more important issue is this: do you expect me to repay anything? Because it looks to me as if you can't actually prove any of it and so I'd be reluctant to let go any of my husband's hard-earned money, no matter how he earned it. What do you say to that?"

For a heartbeat or two, neither Sergeant Bradley nor Constable Cooper said anything. When Elise glanced up to ascertain whether or not they'd been turned to stone – they hadn't – the sergeant was looking pale, whereas the constable was blushing. Goodness me, had she touched a nerve? Perhaps all this 'proof' they were showing her was nothing more than supposition and they were in fact telling her all this in order to provoke some kind of reaction. How very devious! Thank the heavens above that Elise was a connoisseur of *Midsomer Murders* and *Wycliffe* and therefore knew exactly how the police might operate.

Real life was turning out to be more like fiction than she'd supposed. Sergeant Bradley was the first to recover – perhaps by dint of being the senior and more experienced of the two.

"We already know you're innocent," he said. "Our surveillance tells us so in no uncertain terms. Mr. Walker took good care to do everything without your knowledge and, indeed, went out of his way on several occasions to make sure you weren't implicated. There's no need to worry yourself about what might happen in that regard."

He finished his reassurances about Elise's non-criminal status with a broad smile. It did little to comfort her, though she could tell his dental work had been both thorough and successful, which was at least something. If she was going to be arrested at some point, she would definitely wish it to be by a police officer with good teeth.

However, his attitude came over as rather patronising, an attitude which always made her bridle.

Elise turned in her chair and squared up to the man. "I'll have you know," she said, "that I don't appreciate being written off as unworthy of comment, no matter how beneficial the circumstances of being ignored might be. I have no concerns about my innocence of any crime as you'll be pleased to hear my conscience is clear. What worries me more is what your plans are in involving me at all. Is it usual for the police to speak so freely with the wife of an apparently known criminal? It doesn't seem usual to me, though I'm no expert. So, I ask you again: what about Gerald's money?"

This time it was Constable Cooper who answered. Perhaps she was the financial whizz of the pair. "At the moment," the constable said, "everything Gerald leaves to you, Mrs. Walker, is yours. It's not possible to bequeath monies gained from criminal activities to another person in a legal will, not directly. Though, of course, there is the issue of how much of such monies helped to finance your comfortable lifestyle in the first place."

Ah, Elise thought. Here it was at last: the veiled threat, or possibly a warning. It was hard to tell. She smiled, though her smile was – she hoped – not as broad or false as Sergeant Bradley's. "Yes, indeed," she said. "The assets I currently own haven't been accused of being illegal, have they? Therefore all of them will remain with me. It's what my husband would have wanted."

"Of course," the constable continued, nodding as if Elise's fighting answer was nothing more than she'd expected. "There is just the small matter of the searches we will at some point need to carry out. We still need to try to find those vanishing funds."

Elise blinked. "Searches? I'm not sure you'll find any more out from Gerald now he's dead than you did while he was alive. You seem to have all the digital financial know-how at your fingertips already."

"We do." This time it was Sergeant Bradley who took up the baton of the law from his colleague. "But in order to clear up a few things and bring the whole case to a close, we need to ask you if we can search your property in the near future, Mrs. Walker. In case your husband left anything incriminating which might be of use to us."

Elise stood at last and faced them both down. "I see. You'll have to let me think about it," she said. "Because, firstly, I have a funeral to arrange."

## Chapter Five

The one fact Elise took away from Gerald's funeral was that people seemed to assume she would be feeling lonelier than she in fact was. The absence of Gerald lay more lightly on her shoulders than society expected. It was as if, although her marriage had been a good one in her terms – and perhaps Gerald's too – it had somehow reached an end although it was likely neither of them had fully understood it.

Gerald had therefore, in his quiet and intelligent way, died at the right time. It was something of a shame, however, that he'd left behind him such a cloud of mystery. After she'd returned from the police station a couple of weeks ago, Elise had searched the house thoroughly to see if Gerald had left any clues about his life for her to find and which she would never, under any circumstances, allow the police to see. It would also have been useful to have discovered some kind of clue as to where he might have hidden a hundred thousand pounds.

She could certainly think of several items she could spend it on, but it was evidently not to be.

Elise had found nothing. Nothing, apart from the note about the allotment. And she didn't think this had any particular significance. Gerald was, of course, always scribbling things down for no apparent reason and she'd learnt to live with his small and easily forgotten lists. But one thing above all made her feel rather proud; she was already planning to hide things from the law. How simply marvellous! Gerald would surely have been proud too.

In the days between her visit to the police station and the funeral, Elise didn't contact the officers again. Not directly. They'd rung her on the third day, and asked again if it would be possible to arrange a visit. By this, she understood them to mean they would like to search through Gerald's belongings and presumably his computer too. Despite happily using the computer at work, the internet age had passed Elise by at home, but her lack of personal virtual awareness had never bothered her. Such activities were for office life, not for her private life. Still, she supposed she would have to let the police do whatever they wanted to in the end or they'd get a search warrant, or whatever it might be called in real life. Her only criminal references were fictional ones.

So, after lots of prevarication and a surprising few sharp words, Elise had agreed the police could come and do whatever they had to, but on the day after Gerald's funeral. Their parting shot before she ended the call was to request she not tamper with anything until then, either his computer or anything else her husband had owned.

Elise had no intention of tampering. For a start she didn't know Gerald's computer password so couldn't access his files. She did wonder if the password might be 'allotment' but when she tried, it certainly wasn't. So much for that idea. It had always been a very outside chance. And secondly, in terms of physical objects she might 'tamper with', she had no intention of sending any of her husband's belongings to the charity shops just yet. It was far too soon. She may not have been a widow for long, but she knew such activities were reserved until *after* the funeral.

The police, if they truly knew anything, would have known this.

So, in the days between Gerald's death and his funeral, Elise focused on the necessary arrangements, and put the mystery of Gerald to one side. She could deal with it later, but right now she had to think about an astonishing amount of issues she'd never imagined thinking about: what Gerald might like to wear for his final appearance, what sort of coffin he would prefer, the nature of the service and what the wake should be like. The people she spoke to didn't actually use the word 'wake' but Elise liked it and used it whenever she could squeeze it into a sentence. It made her feel more important, and necessary, and nobody queried it. Perhaps it was bad form to correct a widow. Still, it was nice to be unassailably right for once. Being right didn't happen often to a woman in her fifties. In Elise's experience, they were usually deemed wrong in some fashion.

Most of these arrangements, Elise could easily handle. However, the arrival of the local vicar was almost beyond what she thought she should be expected to bear. Neither she nor Gerald had been a churchgoing couple, though whether or not they believed in God was still under consideration. Though probably not for Gerald, any more.

Years ago, Elise had even toyed with the idea of popping in one Sunday to the local church for the odd service, but rumours of its evangelical approach to its Maker had put her off.

Now the priest himself was at her door, offering both sympathy (restrained) and a good church send-off (his words, not hers) for Gerald. She wasn't sure about his commitment, especially as he appeared not to have bothered to brush his hair this morning. Still, in true English female fashion, Elise subdued her criticisms and prepared herself to listen to what he might have to say.

She hoped there wouldn't be much about God, but as he was an Evangelical, she thought her hopes would be dashed. They were.

"I'm so sorry about your loss," Reverend Parker began. "Such a terrible loss for us all, in fact. Gerald was always a great supporter of local charities."

Yes, Elise supposed he had been, though Gerald's attendance at local functions had more to do with the fact people kept asking and he enjoyed an easy life. She'd never gone with him, preferring to stay at home and do nothing. Perhaps this was the hidden agenda behind the vicar's emphasis on Gerald's goodness and not her own. If only he knew what Gerald had really been up to.

"We're all going to miss him," the Reverend continued though Elise hadn't been paying much attention in the last few moments. "Now, at some point soon, you'll need to think about the funeral. I'm happy to say the church is at your disposal, Mrs. Walker, and the church wardens and I are happy to fit you in – I mean Gerald, of course – whenever possible, bearing other church commitments in mind. Wednesdays and Thursdays are the best days, as they're currently the least booked up. And of course, our church choir and band are always happy to perform."

Elise blinked. "Church band?"

"Yes," he nodded eagerly and leant forward as if to impress on her the utter importance of the band. "We have a lot of young people in our church and they're very keen musicians. Talented too. Gerald always seemed to appreciate their performances on the occasions he was free to attend a concert. They would love to give him the send-off he needs."

It was all Elise could do not to laugh out loud. After the two church band concerts Gerald had attended, he'd come back home desperate for a quick whisky and the music of Beethoven in order to cleanse his memory of the experience. No doubt, he'd not put it like that when the vicar had asked his opinion.

The thought of allowing the church band to wreak their particular brand of havoc over Gerald's last rites was almost enough to make her flee from the room. Unless, of course, she agreed purely in order to exercise her right to revenge for Gerald's criminal silence. How tempting it was … though only for a moment. Because, if she allowed the band to do their worst, she'd have to sit through the service and listen to them too.

"No, thank you," she said to the eagerly awaiting but soon to be disappointed priest. "Thank you for enquiring so kindly, but a non-church service is what Gerald would have preferred."

***

True to her words, Elise chose a funeral utterly unconnected with the church or even any kind of crematorium. In the last few months of his life, Gerald had talked about his admiration for natural burials, and so this was what Elise picked for him.

She chose an area of common land not too far away from her village and she made sure the service was as simple and practical as possible. She didn't want any New Age-type nonsense. To Elise's mind, this would be as bad as having an Evangelical church funeral, or nearly so. The joy of a natural burial for Gerald was she was in charge of arranging everything and it catered very nicely to her desire to be in control. This thought made her smile, wryly – it was good to feel as if she were in control of something, at least. Gerald's death had spun everything out of her grasp and she didn't like it one bit.

On the morning of the funeral, she received a bouquet of cream roses – for grief, she imagined, although she was no expert on the language of flowers. It certainly made a pleasant change from a wreath – she was starting to get a little depressed at those. When she opened the card, she saw it was from the office. Instigated by her boss, Hugh, no doubt. He was the kind of man who would think about this sort of social nicety. He'd already telephoned twice and sent a card to offer his condolences. Elise hadn't felt able to talk much but she'd appreciated the conversation they'd had. Soon, very soon, she would need to get back to work and try to carve her life into another kind of shape. She simply had to get the funeral over first, and then she could start to manage everything else.

However, could she rebuild her life properly again in the light of Gerald's criminal existence? She wasn't sure but she knew she would need to know more than the police were willing to tell her.

All that was for later. Today, she had a funeral to attend and, also, a card to read again.

*With every good wish and deepest sympathies, Elise,* the card said. *We're all thinking of you a great deal. From Hugh and the team.*

Exactly what she would have put on his card if the positions had been reversed. Unexpectedly, she found herself smiling, and brushed the reaction away before she committed a serious faux-pas. Surely it wasn't the done thing to smile on the morning of one's husband's funeral, especially if the smile was to do with another man. Still, at least there was nobody around to see it. And it wasn't as if there was anything *of that nature* going on between Hugh and herself. It was simply that she enjoyed working with him and he was a very kind man. She wondered if Hugh might come to the funeral. It would certainly be a support if he did, though of course he'd be busy and she, for once, wasn't at work to support him.

Still, it didn't matter either way, and she wasn't going to ring Hugh and ask him outright. It would be far too embarrassing, for both of them. Besides, she had a very important task to perform, which absolutely needed to be done now. She had to find something to wear.

In her normal, everyday life, Elise was not a huge fan of fashion or its strange vagaries. She liked to wear clothes which were both stylish and comfortable. It was all she asked of her wardrobe, which as a result was small but focused. She possessed clothes for every day of the week for work (with an outfit to spare, just in case of disaster) and a variety of suitable weekend clothes, depending on how she chose to fill the time.

Today was all about Gerald, and she – more than she ever thought she would – needed to find something he would have admired on her. Even though he'd never get to see it.

So Elise retrieved from her one small wardrobe all the suitable outfits she thought Gerald might have appreciated, and laid them out on the bed for her perusal. They didn't need to be black, although some were. Many were blue – Elise was a woman who valued the benefits of blue – and a few were pink. Her celebration outfits, she liked to call them.

She didn't wear those often. With a small sigh, Elise put the pink outfits away. One day, she promised herself, one day …

For a moment or two, her hand hovered over her black offerings, but she shook her head. She wore black when she wanted to be invisible – more invisible than a middle aged, middle class English woman usually was – but she wasn't convinced now was the right time to hide. She needed to 'be there' for Gerald, as the younger people said, so black wouldn't do.

What about green? No, too naturalistic and she might blend in with the background of the woodland setting. That would be a definite mistake, particularly as Elise didn't want to be seen as the kind of woman who would even dream about blending in. It wasn't her way. Invisibility, yes; blending, no. Absolutely not.

Next, Elise considered the red. Something vibrant and fierce, something that would say to whoever considered such fripperies that she, Elise Walker, was in the grip of strong emotion and didn't care who knew it. Exactly what emotion that would be was her own affair, but today of all days it did no harm to indicate its existence.

Yes, the red it would be.

Elise washed quickly, sprayed on deodorant and slipped on the red pencil skirt and matching box jacket. It brushed her still slim hips rather finely, though she said it herself and shouldn't. Under the jacket, she wore a subtly striped pale pink blouse. The whole ensemble would have made Gerald smile, and this was surely what it was all about. What anyone else might think was irrelevant.

The funeral was set for 3pm. Elise reckoned this was enough time both for people to arrive from outside the county, if they so wished, and to get back home afterwards if they needed to. She'd arranged a post-funeral buffet at home – thank goodness for caterers! – but there was no guarantee people would wish to attend or to stay long. She'd made sure the majority of the food was freezable.

Elise arrived half an hour early for the funeral as she wasn't sure what the etiquette might be. This wasn't something she'd thought to ask the Natural Death Organiser before. And it wasn't something the Death Organiser, Mrs. Edrington, had thought to tell her either. Perhaps Elise was simply the kind of woman who looked as if she was always on time. She wouldn't be surprised if this was the impression she gave but, as she approached the small wooden gates of the burial ground, she made a mental note to try to be more unreliable in life.

There might be much to be said for it.

Mrs. Edrington greeted Elise with the sort of calm and compassionate smile which was no doubt second-nature to her. After a few words, the two women made their way through the gate, around the centre and down the path to the woodland where Gerald would be finally laid to rest. Though it was December, nearly Christmas in fact, it wasn't cold and Elise didn't need her warm woollen coat. She could probably make do with just the jacket and scarf. Neither woman spoke, and Elise was glad.

As they arrived at the setting, Elise couldn't help being impressed by the way Mrs Edrington and her team had set up for the service. Or perhaps 'event' would be a better descriptor. Service smacked of too much religion. Neat chairs had been lined up in three gently curving rows, with a gap in the middle. Not too many chairs and not too few. Gerald and she had few friends, but the neighbours – including the ever-helpful Lottie – had said they'd come. And of course he had his business associates. His legitimate ones. Perhaps his less legitimate ones too? Elise would be very interested indeed to meet those. She wondered if they would attend. Were funerals – even natural burial ones – just too normal for criminals?

"I can put more seats out if need be," Mrs. Edrington said, her tone a cornucopia of reassurance. "Some guests have already arrived."

She waved her hand to the right and stepped back so Elise could get a better look at the new arrivals. A group of three men and one woman were standing as far back as possible under the trees. One of the men in the middle – and also the youngest – was dressed entirely in white. On his left were two hulking men dressed in black, and on his right was an equally hulking woman who wore a skirt as if it was something she'd not come across for a while.

Elise instantly liked her.

They didn't look like anyone Gerald had ever introduced her to, so Elise decided to rectify the error right now. She hoped they were the criminals she was planning to meet. She schooled her face to the sort of polite and welcoming expression suitable for a new widow and walked up to the group.

She extended her hand. "Good afternoon. Thank you so much for coming. You must be …"

Elise ran out of words at this point, a concept quite unusual for her. She normally had no trouble expressing herself but the nature of the meeting or what these people called themselves wasn't in her repertoire. Yet.

She needn't have worried.

The man in white extended an elegant and beautifully-manicured hand to take her own. His grip was surprisingly firm.

"We must be Gerald's private business colleagues," he said with a slight smile. "Yes, we understand the police have already spoken with you. I'm Luke, Gerald's Number

Two, and these are Hank, Flank and Janet. Not real names, but it's best not to use those if we can help it. I know there's a lot to talk about, but today we're here to pay our respects to Gerald, and also to you. I'm sorry we have to meet you here for the first time like this, but it was always Gerald's wish to keep his private life and his private business separate."

Yes, Elise thought, he'd certainly succeeded too. She nodded and let go of Luke's hand. "Thank you for coming today," she said again. It was all she could think of.

By then, other people had started to gather, and Elise exchanged a few words with them all, as best she could. Usually, at the other funerals she'd been to, there'd been no conversations until after the burial or cremation was over, but this was her event, and she made the rules. She noticed one or two people glancing over at Luke and his entourage but nobody said anything. This was a relief as Elise wasn't yet sure what kind of response she could make to any direct questions about the strangers.

Five minutes before 3pm, everybody who was coming – or at least everyone she'd assumed would come

– was there. As well as her neighbours and Gerald's (legitimate) work colleagues, she was pleased to see her own work colleagues as well. Hugh, and a couple of work friends who sat nearby in the office, had taken the time to attend, and Elise found herself unexpectedly glad for it. She was especially surprised as a natural burial surely wasn't Hugh's first choice of funeral venue. He was a very traditional kind of man. It was in any case good to have people directly related with her life here, rather than those she and Gerald had shared, and not to mention those only he had known about.

Two minutes before the event was due to start, Elise saw a movement at the corner of her eye. When she turned to peer down the small path to the gate again, she saw the police, in the shape of Sergeant Bradley and Constable Cooper, had arrived.

If Elise had hoped the police might lurk at the back and quietly observe everyone, she was soon proved wrong. The officers walked calmly up the small informal aisle and each shook her hand. As they did so, she became aware of a frisson of movement from Luke and his fellows. It was as if a sudden wind had arrived in their midst and stirred them up. Absolutely the last thing she wanted at Gerald's funeral was a scene, and she hoped the presence of the law wouldn't bring things – whatever those things might be – to a head. Then she told herself not to be so ridiculous. This wasn't a film, this was real life.

She and the police murmured some small talk while she continued to keep a watchful eye on Luke. She sensed an awful lot of shuffling and some muttering too, but thankfully the police ignored it.

"We'll sit at the back, out of the way," Sergeant Bradley said as he quickly came to an end of his pre-funeral chat abilities. "We wanted to pay our respects."

If only Elise could have believed him. Still, at least she had the satisfaction of knowing she'd been right in her initial analysis; the officers wanted to sit at the back to keep an eye on what was going on, including the gangsters. Was 'gangsters' the right word? When she had a chance to speak to Luke once more, she'd be sure to ask him.

As she turned to sit down again, she caught Hugh's eye on the other side of the aisle and smiled. He smiled back, a response that warmed her, and then the service began.

Mrs. Edrington welcomed them, and gave them a brief resume of what would happen. Elise had asked her to do so, as she didn't think many people would know what a natural funeral was. She hated the thought her decisions might cause unnecessary confusion. It was best to aim for clarity at all times.

The plan was this: a short talk from herself, and then other people would be asked to share their memories of Gerald. Afterwards they would listen to a recording of the first movement of Beethoven's sixth symphony. Gerald had always particularly enjoyed it, and so did she. Then the coffin – all of it pleasingly biodegradable – would be buried under one of the trees at the edge of the wood. Finally, she would round up the event and they would return to her house for refreshments.

Gerald would have loved the simplicity and the style, so it was a shame he couldn't be here to enjoy it.

When Elise stood and moved to the front, Mrs. Edrington subtly switched the music off. In all honesty, it had been so subtle Elise hadn't actually noticed it until it was no longer there. Much like Gerald in recent times, then.

She had the unaccountable desire to laugh, which wouldn't have done at all. She had to force herself to think of the necessity of mowing the lawn and checking the myriad engineering features of her car in the future, without the help of her husband, in order to keep a straight face.

She'd best get on with it. As she glanced over the small but perfectly formed crowd, she could see the expectation on their expressions. Soon, if she said nothing, it would rise to a kind of English contained panic in the face of the unknown. That would never do.

"Thank you for coming today," she began, and was astonished to hear how calm she sounded and how at ease with herself. "I very much appreciate it and I'm sure Gerald would too."

A wave of murmured laughter rippled through the crowd, and Elise felt herself relax. It just proved the old adage true: make them laugh and you could get away with most things.

"Gerald was a quiet man," she continued. "But he had his own particular way of doing things and getting things done. And he rarely let opposition get in his way. Not that he made a song and dance about his difficulties, but he simply sidestepped the issues and got on with it. I very much admired that aspect of my husband's personality, though on occasion it could be very frustrating. People often underestimated him, and this could prove a foolish move every so often. Even now."

She paused, smiled and gazed round the mourners. Sergeant Bradley was nodding agreement, while Luke gave her a wry smile in return. Elise took a deep breath before carrying on.

"Because it seems there's a great deal even a wife can't know about her husband," she continued. "As I'm gradually finding out for myself. Perhaps our marriage was – what shall I call it? – very English as it was always very civilised and we took special care not to hurt each other's feelings. At least I like to think so. Gerald, as I've said, was a quiet man. He wasn't a great one in coming forward about his loves or interests. He didn't talk about himself much, but I knew him as a man who was passionate about classical music and gained great joy from his garden. We enjoyed many nights at the theatre together, and he once even helped out behind the scenes at our local drama group, before work – in all its guises – became too busy and too demanding for him. He was a lover of crosswords and crime dramas, the latter of which could never be too dark or too obscure for his tastes. He also enjoyed studying and only two years ago completed an online Theology degree which he told nobody about as he did it purely for the love of studying. He never wanted to be a vicar, and to be honest I never wanted that either."

A further few gentle chuckles here and there, and Elise paused before continuing. "Yes, he was a secretive man in many ways. Indeed, because of this and as I've just told you, there are apparently a few facts about my husband I didn't know about. I have no doubt that the reasons why the police are looking into Gerald's affairs will soon be in our local newspaper, but before that should happen, I did want to say this: Gerald was the kindest man I've ever known, and no doubt ever will know. Whatever he did or did not keep from me, it doesn't matter, because the way he treated me was simply the best throughout all our life together. The kind of good solid team we became through our marriage was something known only to the two of us, but it was something very precious and rare in this world, and I'm honoured to have lived with him for a while. Thank you."

With no further ado, Elise left the front and sat down in her allotted seat. She thought she'd probably said enough. Certainly enough for the assembled people to be taking in, anyway.

A slight pause and then Luke said, quietly but with conviction, "Hear, hear, Mrs. Walker. Hear, hear."

During the ensuing murmurs of what Elise hoped was approval, Mrs. Edrington rose. "Thank you, Mrs. Walker. If anyone would like to say a few words about Mr. Walker before we listen to some of his favourite music, then please do feel free. You don't have to come up to the front, but it would be helpful if you could stand where you are and speak so the rest of us can hear you."

Elise thought that at this point, there'd be a very English pause before someone found the courage to get up, but in fact three people instantly stood up: Luke; Sergeant Bradley; and – of all people – Hugh.

She nodded at Luke to go forward first, as all three men looked towards her for guidance. Elise had never known herself to have any power at all in a public setting, and she found she rather enjoyed it.

She was also very keen to see what Luke had to say. As the fair-haired man made his way to the front, one of his bodyguards following him closely, Sergeant Bradley looked as if he might be about to object to her choice, but Constable Cooper laid a calming hand on his sleeve and he subsided into his chair. Good to know at least one of the police officers understood the value of manners, Elise thought.

She turned her attention to Luke. The bodyguard – she didn't know which one it was – had taken a couple of steps back but was still glancing around as if a threat might suddenly materialise from the woods. Evidently he took his job very seriously indeed. Elise could admire his approach.

"Most of you don't know me," Luke began, which was as true a statement as Elise had heard in a while. "And that may well be a mark in your favour, though such discussions are certainly not for today. Because today is a sad day for me and for my colleagues. We've known Gerald for many years and he's always been an example of industry, subtlety and cunning for us in our careers and indeed our lives. He's been a man we've always admired and trusted, which in our line of work is a definite and unexpected bonus. I'm sorry to say that because of a variety of circumstances it's only today we've been able to meet his wife, Elise Walker, and it's been a pleasure to make her acquaintance. I hope we can build on that relationship in the future and share memories of Gerald together. It's something I very much look forward to. Thank you."

Speech over, Luke nodded in Elise's direction and walked back to his seat. The bodyguard with him had obviously expected his boss to speak for a little longer and had to trot after Luke in order to catch up.

As Elise watched them both return to their seats, she didn't need to wonder why Luke had kept things brief, as she could see the scowl on Sergeant Bradley's face. Elise understood only too well how Luke's words had been full of his own personal – and no doubt criminal – agenda, but she hadn't expected the police to read so much into his statement about the budding relationship between herself and Gerald's gang too. More fool her then. Everyone wanted to know where the money was, whichever side of the law they had chosen. She'd best keep her wits about her from now on. And she'd best let the police speak too, so she smiled at Sergeant Bradley with bright expectation.

He got the message, and stood to make his speech in turn. Unlike Luke, he stayed where he was, however. Perhaps he felt there would be more safety amongst the crowd. Though, in all honesty, Elise thought it unlikely there would be any actual physical violence. There were independent witnesses and, besides, this was Surrey. Violence, if it occurred, would be carried out verbally, and the damage would be internal.

Sergeant Bradley coughed before speaking, which Elise thought was a little too near a cliché but she schooled her face to avoid disapproval. This was a funeral not a wedding – and so disapproval had no place here.

"Many of you may be surprised to see the police at Mr. Walker's funeral," he began. "But we have always taken an interest in Mr. Walker's business affairs and so it seemed discourteous not to attend. It's good to see so many friends of the family here today. You might wish to know that in the days ahead we'll no doubt be visiting you and getting to know you a little better. For now, I'd just like to say we'll miss Mr. Walker more than you can imagine. Because of him, my colleague Constable Cooper here, and I are far more astute and experienced at our jobs than we otherwise would be. Mr. Walker was a very clever, challenging and occasionally frustratingly cunning man, and our world will be the poorer now he's gone. He leaves his mark on us all. Thank you."

When Sergeant Bradley sat down, there was a moment's silence and then the soft hum of surprised conversation. Well, Elise thought, if Gerald's criminal career had to come out, then his funeral was as good a place as any for it to do so. When she glanced at Mrs Edrington, however, it was evident this wasn't her idea of a seemly occasion, as the frown between her eyes could have cut wood.

Luckily Hugh slipped past Elise, wafting a faint spice of aftershave in his wake, and made his way to the front. He nodded once at her before he began speaking and the gesture gave Elise an extraordinary feeling of comfort.

"I didn't know Gerald directly," Hugh began. "I've worked closely with Elise at the University for three years, and I only really know him through her. But I've always thought their marriage was a very solid one. Certainly far more than mine ever was – I'm divorced, sadly – and I came to admire their understated confidence and loyalty towards each other. It gave me hope. So, whatever may happen in the future and whatever might be discovered about him now, it's important to remember Gerald Walker was a good husband to Elise and therefore – in my view – a good man. Thank you."

He sat down. Elise found she was blinking away tears at his words. Somehow, they meant more than all the other speeches, even her own, and more than the service itself.

She rose to her feet once more. "Thank you, Hugh," she said, her voice a little unsteady. "And to Luke and the police as well. It's always good to know as much about a person as we can, and to get a rounded picture of them. If anyone else would like to say anything, you'd be most welcome."

After that, the normal flow of a funeral – whatever that might be – seemed to reinstate itself in some measure, as several people stood and spoke a few kind words about Gerald. Finally, the gathered people sat or stood in thoughtful silence for the rest of the planned schedule. Nothing else untoward took place, and Gerald was fittingly laid to rest in his biodegradable but not too cheap coffin under a young oak tree, and the service at last was done.

The post-service refreshments would, Elise hoped, be less quietly fraught. For one thing, she intended to have a very good conversation with Luke and his gang. Did that make her the gangster's wife? The thought made Elise snort. She wasn't half as glamorous as she should be then, if she was going to claim such a title. She was neither blonde nor big-bosomed, nor young, and had no desire to be any of these. Besides, by rights it should be the gangster's widow, shouldn't it?

Such thoughts were still shifting through her head when she arrived home twenty minutes later to find the caterers had already set everything exactly as she wanted it. Good to know there was one aspect of today she had no need to worry about. Elise promised herself she would tip the caterers and tip them well.

This was all the clarity of thought she had time for before the mourners arrived. With them came a long and really quite exhausting series of clichéd statements, the like of which Elise thought she would take some time to recover from. Not that she could fault the outpouring of compassionate sympathy from the majority of guests. In the past, she would have done exactly the same at any funeral, however well or badly she knew the deceased. It was what was expected by tradition, and tradition could be an exacting master.

Still, it was wearying, as indeed was schooling her face into the same brave but strong expression Elise imagined she should be wearing. She had already made the decision not to cry. There had been a flutter of tears earlier on, mainly in response to what Hugh had said, but she wanted no more.

In the midst of sandwiches and polite sympathy at her situation, Elise still found time to accost the police.

"What do you think?" she said to Sergeant Bradley as he refilled his plate with at least four salmon sandwiches. "Will Gerald's less than legitimate colleagues start searching my home for the loot whilst his coffin is still warm? Or is this what you're hoping to do while I'm being the maitresse d'?"

A choking noise to one side and Elise turned to see Constable Cooper struggling to keep the mouthful of fruit juice contained within her lips. Sergeant Bradley gave her a harsh stare before plastering on a smile for Elise. His plate of sandwiches wobbled precariously on the edge. Elise knew exactly how it felt.

"I hope they won't, Mrs. Walker," the officer replied. "We're here to make sure fair play happens. Though, as you've mentioned the issue of the money, might I ask once again if there is a convenient time for us to have a careful look around your house and property? You promised us after the funeral, if you remember. We'll leave everything just as we found it, naturally. You'll hardly notice we're here."

Later, Elise thought it had perhaps been something of a cheek to ask her to agree to a police search at her dead husband's funeral party, but she couldn't fault Sergeant

Bradley's dedication to his task. And she was always an admirer of dedication, in any form.

So she'd suggested the very next day, not imagining the police would be in any way ready. But she'd underestimated the planning skills of the law, as her suggestion was quickly confirmed and a time agreed upon. It seemed a little soon but, in any case, she was due back at work next week, and would definitely prefer to have the police visitation over with before then. She needed to get on with her life. Was it strange she was thinking such thoughts before Gerald's remains were properly cold? Once more, she could have done with knowing about the etiquette of mourning, but then again she tended to be happiest carving out her own path.

Interesting though that, by the time the funeral refreshments had been consumed or cleared away and the last guests had departed, Elise had still not had an opportunity to speak to Luke. It would have to remain a pleasure deferred.

## Chapter Six

In the morning, Elise rose late and took a long bath, allowing the scent of lemongrass to prepare her for the day. The police and their teams weren't due until 10.30am and she felt sure she would have to be at her strongest while she endured them. The caterers of the day before had more than carried out their duties and there was very little to tidy up. She almost felt redundant, but then again it was one less matter to concern her.

Was tidying for the police something to consider or would they think she was hiding terrible secrets? Elise couldn't help but smile to herself as she prepared her morning cereal and coffee. If only she knew what she was supposed to be hiding, she would certainly do so. It would – if he'd had the time to express himself before death took him – surely have been what Gerald would have wanted. It was no less than her marital duty.

A sudden thought took her and she reached for her handbag lying sulkily on the dining room floor. She took out her purse and found the scribbled message in Gerald's handwriting.

*Allotment.*

Elise frowned, again. His last message. Was it a clue? If it was, how she wished Gerald had been more direct in his desire to convey information – though of course it was not his way. He had never been the most communicative of men, which to Elise's mind had been one of his many strengths. Too much communication was a curse – a lifetime in her office career had told her as much. In any case, Gerald didn't have an allotment. He referred to his vegetable patch at the side of the house as his 'allotment' on occasions, so perhaps he'd hidden something there?

If she had the energy or the time before the arrival of the law, she supposed she should have been digging up the raised beds like a woman possessed, but she had neither the time nor energy. Anyway, the police would do this – it was their job.

She'd be curious to see what they found – if rather more than slightly regretful they wouldn't allow her the use of any discovered cash. She also wondered how they would put her garden back to rights if they dug it up. It would be something she would keep a very watchful eye on indeed.

Because, for all her faults and she was sure there were many, Elise loved her garden. She would be cross if it was ruined. The police wouldn't appreciate her reaction. She would make sure of it.

By the time the police arrived, one minute after 10.30am, Elise was as ready as possible. She opened the door before they could knock. Always best to be one step ahead in all situations.

As expected, officers Bradley and Cooper were in the lead. Behind them was a veritable team of police more numerous than Elise had expected. Just how many people did it take to search an average-sized Surrey home?

"Goodness," she said. "You do have a lot of friends, don't you? I should have bought another packet of biscuits."

Sergeant Bradley reddened. "It's the standard search team, Mrs. Walker. Please may we come in?"

Without further ado, Elise stepped to one side and beckoned them across the threshold. She counted ten young men, not including the officers she knew, where she'd only expected five. All of them were in fact men, apart from Constable Cooper. Perhaps house searches weren't something female police officers were interested in. A shame really, as Elise would definitely have chosen it as a career strand if she'd ever wanted to be in the police. What could be nicer than looking round people's houses and discovering all about their lives?

Mind you, perhaps she would have been better off paying more attention to her husband and discovering *his* life. She might have been a far wiser woman now if she'd bothered to do so then. Oh well. It was too late. She would simply have to turn her attentions to discovering her husband after his death, rather than before.

Such a decision would have given Gerald cause for a quiet smile. And she couldn't have blamed him for it.

While the police did whatever police needed to do before they started searching the house, Elise made tea. The other alternative was standing in the hallway and screaming at them to be careful of her precious belongings and to understand that for her Gerald had been a very suitable and enjoyable husband and not the criminal mastermind they'd believed him to be.

If she did so, it wouldn't go down well. Screaming and getting *very* angry wasn't expected from a middle-aged, middle-class woman in the heart of Surrey, and the police – not to mention the neighbours – wouldn't be able to cope.

Besides, it would be most exhausting for her, so she only made the tea. The police, while they worked, were unexpectedly quiet. Elise was anticipating more noise and hubbub, or at the very least a low level of chat. However, they worked in silence and only spoke to say thank you when she distributed the required numbers of teas, coffees and biscuits.

She'd thought, briefly, about cake, but decided against it. Gerald wouldn't have approved of her providing any luxury item for the strangers trying to get to the bottom of his secrets. After all, she'd never got to the bottom of them either, and she was no stranger.

She hoped they'd discover enough to leave her alone and not enough that she might be disadvantaged. Though you could never tell nowadays, could you? Perhaps

Officers Bradley and Cooper would squirrel away any of Gerald's ill-gotten gains and decamp to Barbados or wherever people went when they were on the run. After which, she would be left to bemoan her fate to the press, whilst tearfully clutching a picture of the dear departed to her bosom. It was a shame Elise didn't actually have much of a bosom – she was made in the willowy fashion. Perhaps the press could enhance the picture?

A voice at her elbow interrupted her wild imaginings. "Excuse me, Mrs. Walker?"

Elise gasped and swung round. Constable Cooper stood in the doorway of the kitchen. She was glad mind-reading wasn't one of the police's talents. "Yes? What can I do for you?"

"Please could you turn on the computer so we can access it? You've just got the one, have you?"

Elise nodded. "Yes. It was Gerald's. I'm not a fan of computers – I have to deal with them enough at work. I like to relax at home."

The constable nodded but made no reply. Elise wondered if the officer was storing up her words for future accusations, but told herself not to be so dramatic. In

Gerald's office, Elise switched on the computer and stood back to let the officers do their work. The man at the machine seemed very young to her, but perhaps all policemen were like that. No doubt, he couldn't see her at all, as she was above the age of twenty-five. Far far above.

"Do you have the password?" Constable Cooper asked her.

Elise couldn't help a wry smile. "You mean you're not intending to hack into Gerald's online life here when you've already done it from your own offices while you were investigating him? Besides, surely you know the password already if everything you've said to me before is true."

The constable had the grace to blush. "We didn't need the password when we were investigating your husband," she said quietly. "And, yes, we could do as you've suggested. But I thought it would be polite, and quicker, to ask you first."

This time it was Elise's turn to redden. It was a courtesy she'd not expected and which she certainly shouldn't complain about. Still she had no option but to shake her head. "Thank you, but I'm sorry. I simply don't know it."

Constable Cooper shrugged. "Okay. We'll have to hack it then. Harry?"

The young man at the computer – Harry, evidently – nodded, turned and got to work without a word. By the look of it, this might take some time, so Elise, despite her curiosity as to her husband's goings-on, decided to leave.

She walked downstairs and into the garden. Her refuge. It had never been a large garden and of course as it was December, none of the funeral party of yesterday had ventured outside. Such niceties had never stopped Elise. Going outside in winter was what cardigans or jackets were for, and there was always the gloves or hat option. Because she was middle-aged and a naturally cautious woman, however, Elise chose both.

Although the garden was small, part of the reason Elise and Gerald had chosen it was the glorious view over the fields and open countryside. It was almost like having a garden one didn't have to maintain – which was to Elise a plus point although Gerald had never stopped wanting more land. He had been a great believer in the benefits of land even though, when asked, he remained uncertain as to what he would do with it.

Mind you, she pondered, if he'd been able to use his apparently ill-gotten gains, perhaps he would have hired staff to look after the land for him. Gerald would have been very happy indeed at the concept of a domestic empire – he'd often said he had no power at home with herself as his wife. Elise had of course disagreed. It was her view that in a marriage power belonged to the party who spoke less often, and that would have been Gerald.

In the end they had, amicably enough, agreed to disagree. They were good at that.

Elise turned left, made her way along the winding gravel path and sat at the love seat next to the shrubbery. She chose the left hand seat as she always did, and then tutted at herself. Gerald wasn't here now so she could sit wherever she liked. So, because she could, Elise rose, and sat on the right instead, in Gerald's seat.

It didn't feel comfortable. And the view from his seat wasn't as good as the view from hers – she couldn't even see the rose bushes. Still, out of sheer cussedness, she sat for a few minutes before decamping back to the familiar. There was something to be said for routine. Here and now, when everything was very strange indeed, routine had a great deal more to be said for it.

While she waited for the police to do their best, or more accurately, their worst, Elise gazed across the garden and thought again about Gerald, and their marriage. The garden was simple yet somehow it worked, much like themselves and their relationship.

Immediately in front of her lay the shrubbery. It had been part of the design created by the people who'd owned the house before them, but she and Gerald had decided to keep it as it was, though they'd added to it over the years. Currently, it consisted of two spiraeas, a choisya, and two differently coloured lavenders, alongside dwarf buddleias, alliums and two evergreen shrubs whose identity was unknown, though Elise had always loved the structure they provided. Gerald had asked her if they should research what they actually were, but she'd declined the offer. She didn't need to know everything about them – it was enough that the unknown shrubs worked in the space where they found themselves and were easy on the eye.

Perhaps there was a lesson there about Elise's idiosyncratic approach to her marriage, but whether it was a positive or negative lesson she couldn't yet tell. Time, no doubt, would – as it invariably did – reveal all.

To the left of where Elise sat was the flower bed she named her 'happy corner'. It was the only part of the garden created entirely from annuals and Elise dedicated it to any flower that made her smile. On the whole, this consisted of sunflowers, pansies and violas, although every now and again, she spiced up the mix with a lily or two. There was something about the gentle haze of yellow interspersed here and there with a dash of mauve which made everything seem more bearable. Even now and even today.

Behind the love-seat was a line of small trees – or large shrubs depending on your point of view. Underneath them, the primulas winked upwards and courageously through the gloom. Elise could never resist a primula and was always overjoyed when one or two of them even bloomed in the autumn, as well as in the spring. Of course, today they were just a sea of green leaves, but they held deep within them the promise of another season and another year. She hoped she could learn from that kind of faith for her own life.

To her right was the rhododendron, holding its secrets all through winter until it could be fully confident about the spring. And beyond her seat lay the lawn, Gerald's pride. He'd always valued the crisp green stripe effect which adorned the grass all summer long. Elise wondered if she had the energy to carry on his tradition, or whether she'd simply lay the whole expanse out to wildflowers. She liked the thought of a wildflower meadow, though Gerald had always pursed his lips and shaken his head at the very notion of 'weeds.'

It had made Elise laugh and give in to him, but she thought she could do what she liked now, couldn't she? Heavens though, if she couldn't quite bring herself to sit on his side of the love-seat, then she was highly unlikely to begin her mourning period by sowing a wildflower meadow. Her conscience would prick against her.

The lawn idled along the back of the house and then stopped, giving way to Gerald's vegetable plot which swooped round beyond the far side of the living room.

She was about to consider the raised beds – and Gerald – when a voice from the dining room outside door called for her attention.

"Mrs. Walker?"

When she looked up, Elise could see one of the police team trying to attract her attention. A lurch in her heart almost made her topple as she stood. Had they found some evidence of where Gerald had secreted the money? If so, could she keep any of it?

"There's someone to see you," the officer continued before slipping away so Elise could catch sight of the woman standing behind him. It was Lottie from next door and she was holding a tin as if it contained precious jewellery.

Elise had the sudden and quite ridiculous thought that perhaps this tin was where Gerald had stashed the goods – or whatever the phrase was – and was overtaken by an urgent desire to laugh. She swallowed it down for the sake of appearances.

"Lottie, lovely to see you. Thank you so much for coming," Elise began to say as she beckoned her neighbour out into the garden. Well, it wasn't too cold, and Lottie was wearing a jacket that looked warm enough.

She would have said more, but by then Lottie had stepped forward and hugged her with one arm. The other, Elise presumed, was keeping a tight hold on the tin, but she couldn't actually see so she wasn't sure. Funny how it had been so long since anyone but Gerald had held her – and that seldom and not often without asking – that Elise wasn't entirely sure what to do. She was probably too English for hugging to come naturally – she no doubt needed to be French.

As a halfway measure and a sop to the European Union, Elise put one cautious hand round her neighbour's back and gave her a gentle squeeze. Thankfully it seemed to be enough. Lottie let go and Elise was quick to follow the lead.

Lottie swung the tin round and waved it at chest level. "I didn't know what to do when I saw the police were round – and I know you think I'm probably here because I'm terribly nosy but I didn't think you'd want to be on your own – if you were. So here's some cake and you can tell me to go if you want. It's no problem, honestly."

Elise couldn't help but smile. She wasn't used to such directness in her life – Gerald had always been a subtle man who needed to be approached with great cunning. So, at a whim, she gestured for Lottie to join her at the love-seat. "It's not too cold, is it?"

"Oh no. We've been lucky this December, haven't we?" Lottie replied before blushing. "Weather-wise, I mean. Not in every case."

Elise had to agree. "No, you're right. Not in every case."

She was glad to find Lottie parked herself on the right side of the seat, so Elise could take up her usual position. It definitely felt more comfortable having someone there, even though it wasn't Gerald, or even a man, if it came to it. Perhaps she wasn't as cut out for being on her own as she thought. Something to ponder.

For a few moments, the two women sat in silence, and Elise more than appreciated Lottie's courtesy. If their positions had been reversed, she would have wanted to ask a hundred questions, at the very least. She felt honour-bound therefore to offer some kind of explanation to her neighbour.

"I imagine you're wondering why the police are here," she said, gazing ahead at the shrubbery and beyond. "I suppose you must have thought the funeral was strange – poor Gerald, though perhaps he might have enjoyed the tension. Who can say? Certainly not me. I'm not actually sure why everything's suddenly so difficult, beyond what I anticipate would be the normal reaction to losing a husband. I also don't understand quite why the local press aren't leaping on the story with shouts of glee, but they could be biding their time, I suppose. Anyway, the upshot is the police believe Gerald was a white-collar criminal who siphoned off a lot of money over the years from his business dealings. He worked with other criminals, some of whom you might have met at the funeral. They were the ones who looked most like gangsters, as far as Surrey has gangsters.

"Anyway, the police are missing some of the money they've been tracking. A hundred grand, to be exact. So they're searching the house for clues. I don't know what they might find or what it will mean, though I have to admit I'm curious. I suppose it's not every day a woman discovers the husband she thought she was married to isn't actually the man she assumed he was. It's something I'm going to have to come to terms with, for good and bad. So there you have it: the reason for my home being taken apart and, I hope, put back together again by the police."

Elise was planning to say more – much more – now that the words appeared to be so easy to find. But she suddenly found she was crying. Not in an hysterical manner – perish the thought – but the tears simply fell and kept on falling.

She let them. Even though they startled her. Besides she couldn't for the life of her have found the power to stop. All the pent up anger, grief and frustration resulting from Gerald's death and secret life – perish the man indeed! – flowed out at last. She hadn't even realised she'd been suppressing all this quite so much. She had just thought she was being reasonable and calm under difficult circumstances. But apparently she was also human – a factor she hadn't managed to include in the equation of loss. She included it now.

Halfway through her crying fit, she realised Lottie was holding her gently and murmuring soothing sounds. This was at the same time very silly and very comforting. How did some women know how to do this when she herself wouldn't have had the first idea? Another lesson of etiquette she must have missed at school – alongside how to be a girl, the importance of shoes and having the right attitude.

The thought she'd somehow made all the wrong decisions in life made her cry again – and then she cried because she was crying for the wrong reasons. She tried to explain some of this to Lottie, but no doubt Lottie was too nice a person to understand much of Elise's ramblings. Which was a very good thing for future social occasions in the street, as she was sure her rantings wouldn't go down well, and Elise didn't want to be the one to break up the happy local circle.

Or perhaps Gerald's perfidy had already achieved that end? She couldn't imagine the other neighbours would approve of the regular presence of the police in their midst. This was a good neighbourhood and a peace-loving village. At least, on the surface. Though who knew what terrible crimes were being committed out of sight of prying eyes? Look at what Gerald had managed to achieve … Maybe, after all, he wasn't the worst of them.

After a while, Elise stopped crying as even she had run out of tears. Lottie stopped murmuring whatever comforts she was saying and slid back into her section of the seat again. Instead of a raft of questions – which Elise didn't think she could answer – Lottie opened the tin and offered Elise its contents.

"Cake?" her neighbour said. "I always find it's good for a crisis, whatever the crisis may be."

It was lemon drizzle cake. Elise's favourite and a very pleasant coincidence indeed. She took a slice, smiled her thanks and bit in to the welcome gift. It was delicious.

"Thank you," she said in surprise. "If anything could cure the world's problems, then it's probably going to be this."

"Good," said Lottie. "I like to think I'm of some use every now and again."

And then the two women laughed in unexpected companionship and ate their cake in a good kind of silence. After they'd finished, Elise told her with a greater measure of reason everything that had happened since Gerald's unfortunate demise. It didn't take long but it was intense and ran deep. Some things should.

When she'd finished, Lottie didn't immediately respond. Elise wondered if she ought to have offered her a coffee or tea, but the time for that had long since passed. Eventually Lottie said something, but it wasn't what Elise had expected.

"Husbands. They're never what we think they are, are they? Everyone has a secret life, but I have to say yours takes the biscuit, doesn't it? You obviously have hidden depths, Elise."

"Why do you say that?"

"Because if your husband was the complicated and possibly criminal man you now think he is, he would never have wanted to stay married to a simple woman, would he?"

Elise blinked. No, she didn't think he would.

## Chapter Seven

The next working day, Elise returned to the office. The police hadn't found what they wanted to find and had gone away less than pleased. It didn't worry her. What did worry her was the fact they'd not been as tidy in putting everything back in the house and the garden how she wanted it, as they'd promised. So she'd spent a long time making sure everything was just so.

A tidy house was a tidy mind, Gerald had always said. Or was it the other way round? She'd never truly listened to old sayings. Why bother repeating an adage when you'd already said it? It was a mystery.

Not quite so much a mystery as the conversation she'd had with Sergeant Bradley just before the police team had left. She'd been so near to being free of them all, however temporarily, when he'd taken a gentle hold of her arm and steered her into the kitchen which had been the nearest room at the time.

Elise didn't think he wanted to complain about the quality of her tea. Neither did she appreciate being manhandled in such a manner, albeit courteously. Before she could say anything to the point though, he let go. Wise man.

"Before we leave, Mrs. Walker," he said. "Before we leave, I need to ask you if you yourself have seen anything suspicious or which seems out of place. Sometimes, the wife is the best source of information in such cases."

Indeed, Elise was sure that was so, in cases where the wife had had the first inkling of what had been going on in the first place. She didn't like being reminded of her apparent dimness. She opened her mouth to say so and then, from nowhere, the image of Gerald's odd note in the hallway came to her mind: *Allotment*.

She closed her mouth again, and Sergeant Bradley gave her a curious stare. "Mrs Walker? Is there anything you need to tell us? Anything at all?"

Any woman in the world would want to help the police and do whatever they could to ease the wheels of justice. But Elise wasn't any woman, and she'd already made her decision as to whose side she was on. She smiled.

"I don't know anything, do I? As you keep reminding me. So, as far as I'm aware, there's nothing I need to tell you."

"Nothing?"

Goodness, that note must surely be burning the proverbial hole in her handbag by now. "No, nothing. I'm sorry."

She was obviously a better liar than she'd imagined, as Sergeant Bradley's expression cleared, and he nodded. "All right. We're sorry to have disturbed you, and thank you so much for your time, and for allowing us into your home."

Elise hadn't been aware she'd had a choice. As he reached her front door, she couldn't resist one parting shot at the law.

"Oh, there is just one thing," she murmured.

Sergeant Bradley swung round, the light of expectation and – no doubt – his hoped-for glittering career ahead – in his eyes. She smiled sweetly. "I do hope you don't ever need to come back," she said.

And, with that, she utterly and entirely spoke the truth.

Right now, however, she was in the office, where there were so many suspicious or out-of-place events that Sergeant Bradley would be in his element.

Elise worked as a secretary at her local university. Over the last twenty years, her hours had reduced from full-time to three days per week over a series of budget-saving missions. Gerald had been almost furious on her behalf and advised her to fight for her rights, but Elise wasn't a career-minded woman and she wasn't bothered about the money. She'd simply agreed to whatever the powers that be had asked of her. It made for a quieter, more unengaged life, but one she appreciated.

The office kitchen, on the other hand, was a place of mystery and deeply inset hierarchy. When Elise had first arrived in the Registry, she'd noted there were two kettles and for the first few days had been happy to use either of them to make her morning tea or her afternoon coffee. She was always a creature of routine. Then on day four of her tenure, a tall man she'd not yet been introduced to took her to one side and frowned.

He coughed. "I'm terribly sorry, but you work for the Registry, don't you?"

"Yes, I do," she was happy to confirm. Though she wasn't sure why he would have to be sorry about it, whoever he was.

"Then you shouldn't be using the kettle on the right hand side of the kitchen." He gestured to it, as if she wouldn't understand which kettle he might mean. "That's Planning's kettle. Your kettle – the Registry kettle – is the one on the left. The same goes for all the other kitchen items – the tea-towels, the mugs and the plates. The ones on the left are yours and the ones on the right are ours. Do you see?"

Elise nodded. She did see, entirely and absolutely she did. The kitchen was an area of the office divided with as much rigour as the land around the Gaza strip. She could only be thankful she'd not started an inter-departmental war by dint of her unwitting actions. She blinked and tried not to laugh. It took an immense effort. One thing did puzzle her further however.

"I see. Thank you for letting me know. But what about the fridge?" She gestured at it too, in case her colleague needed to be guided towards it. "The fridge is on the right, in your Planning area, but we all use it, don't we?

Planning and Registry people alike. Or did I put my lunch on the wrong shelf today? I'm happy to move it, if that's the case. Do tell."

She gazed at the man, name still unknown. He gazed back. He frowned further as if trying to decipher whether she might have been sarcastic or not. To be honest, Elise herself wasn't sure. Her frame of mind could quite easily have moved from sarcasm to despair at this point. Finally, he blinked and stepped back, all but knocking against the fridge in question.

"No, it's fine," he said. "The fridge is used by everyone."

A neutral zone then, she thought, but didn't say. "Thank you."

Then she quietly took her mug away from the right hand kettle and placed it next to the left hand one. Where it and she evidently belonged. By the time the water had boiled and she'd filled her mug, the man had gone.

Was everyone here mad? It was a high possibility.

The Registry was indeed a strange and complex place. During the last restructure, she'd been given a desk here, even though she and Hugh worked at the time for

Student Services, not the Registry. It had been the only desk available which was relatively near to Hugh. Interestingly, Hugh himself wasn't anywhere near the Student Centre which was situated in the middle of campus, opposite the Careers Service. He was, considered the Powers That Be, far too important to be placed in the Centre he was ultimately in charge of. The Centre was looked after by the Centre Manager, a slim, balding man called Carl who always appeared slightly startled whenever Elise was around. Perhaps this was the effect she had on men? Her personality and general way of being in the world had never seemed to bother Gerald. Then again, he'd had secrets of his own.

Anyway, Hugh's role was strategic, whereas Carl's role as the manager was operational. Or so the official explanation would have them believe. There had been more explanation given to her when she first arrived in the Registry, but Elise hadn't been able to take most of it in. She'd always been allergic to the word 'strategy' and was obliged to have a calming cup of tea and a lie-down, if possible, whenever she heard it. Her overriding feeling was that 'strategy' was nothing more than a managerial attempt to make a simple thing more complicated and important in order to fool the masses. Well, the masses weren't fooled, or rather she certainly wasn't. What they really meant was the vital necessity of having a plan and doing it.

Moreover, when it came to everyone discussing their 'vision and brand', Elise had to close her eyes and think about something else. There was far too much talking in the world and much of it took place in educational establishments.

Sometimes she wondered when the students had time for any learning at all, what with the staff being so busy branding their strategy or realigning their vision. Still, the students didn't have too much to do with the way the administrative departments were run – something they should be everlastingly grateful for – and therefore had more time for the life of the mind. Lucky them.

Still, turning back to her first day here, Elise had expected someone in the Registry team to talk to her on her arrival, but in fact they hadn't. Not until about 4pm on Day Two had one of the older women finally smiled and asked how she was getting on. The way she'd been feeling by then, Elise could have flung her arms around the unsuspecting woman and kissed her, right there in the middle of the silent office. Which just goes to show that even strong-minded, rational women could become lonely at work.

Thankfully, if only for her own peace of mind, Elise hadn't responded in such dramatic kind, and had instead smiled with quiet enthusiasm right back and said she was fine, thank you. It had been enough to break the mysterious ice and, from that moment, the Registry around her had proved to be quite a chatty place, if given to great swathes of quietness, which Elise didn't mind at all. She was given to great swathes of silence herself, she just didn't like to publicise it too much.

Later she'd learnt her and her boss's arrival on the Registry floor – when neither of them belonged to the Registry – had sent deeply-felt shock waves through the office teams. Nobody had explained anything to them and so they had apparently been worried she and Hugh were there to streamline the system even further and take people's jobs away from them.

This realisation had almost made Elise laugh out loud. She couldn't think of any two people least likely to be cast in the roles of office Grim Reaper than she or Hugh. They weren't the culling types. Hugh was too kind-hearted and she was in effect too disinterested in the life of the university to want to make any drastic difference to it. Even though she didn't much like the way business was done here, she wasn't involved enough in either her head or her heart to want to instigate change.

Management would say she didn't have enough 'vision' if they knew the truth of it, but Elise herself would say she had too much humanity and didn't want to lose it. It was the difference between them.

Her boss, Hugh, called her in the moment he saw her at her desk at the start of the week after the funeral. "Elise. It's good to see you. Once again, I'm so sorry about Gerald. Are you sure you want to be here?"

"Thank you. Yes, I'm sure."

He nodded, but still looked uncertain. "All right. But if you feel you need to leave, then it's fine. But I'm glad you're here. I can certainly do with the help. Thank you for making the effort."

Elise smiled, and was still smiling when she sat down at her desk and started sorting through the scattered paperwork across her keyboard. How she wished people would at least stack work neatly. She hated to have an untidy desk, and especially if the untidiness wasn't of her own volition.

It was, however, amusing how Hugh imagined she'd come in purely to please him and his work demands – which were many and varied and always seemed to assume she was at her desk for the full five days and not for only three. She'd learnt to live with it.

In fact, she'd come in for her own reasons – because she had no wish to mope around the house and because she needed to start her own life without Gerald. He had thrown a shadow of criminality over her existence with his death, but she was determined to claw back a measure of her own life too. Work was familiar, somewhere she could do her job and yet have space in her mind to think things through to her own satisfaction.

Thinking things through was what Elise prided herself on, and she was determined not to give up the habit just because she was now a widow. She hadn't changed after all; it was merely that Gerald had left her.

So, while her mind ranged across a variety of cogent topics, Elise dealt with the papers and emails – and more importantly the demands behind them – which her working life was so very full of. Hugh had six months ago been moved to the new post of Deputy Registrar, away from Student Support, but she was still his PA. The two of them had had a great deal to do when the post had been created, and they still had a great deal to do today.

She'd been away from the University for a matter of weeks, which was surely long enough for someone to deal with her correspondence, real and virtual. However, her hopes of such a miracle when everyone else was busy to the point of no return remained unrealised. Her email inbox was full of requests and statements, most of which she knew from long experience would be meaningless. Sometimes, Elise remembered back when computers had first been introduced to the working world during an earlier similar job of hers. All those years ago, the Vice-Chancellor of the time had given a speech saying they were now putting one foot onto the Information Highway, and as a result their working lives would soon be far easier and there would be a lot more leisure time for them all. What nonsense the man had talked! These days Elise knew perfectly well that the arrival of the Internet had meant they all worked far harder and – or so it seemed to her – for far lesser purpose. Nobody ever paid any real attention when she said so however; they simply laughed and scuttled back to their computer screens.

For this reason, Elise had no Twitter or Facebook or YouTube accounts, and only rarely turned on her mobile phone – a present from Gerald which she had not asked for. Such lack of connection enabled her to retain the necessary sense of herself and she never regretted it.

So, once more, Elise squared her shoulders for the working day and began to sift her emails, deleting the irrelevant ones, answering those expressing condolence for her loss and dealing with the ones involving an actual response. It kept her busily if not happily occupied for an hour or so. The hour was interspersed with colleagues drifting like snowflakes to her desk and offering their regret at Gerald's passing. Or death, as Elise preferred to call it. Passing sounded far too elegant and Gerald, for all his plus points, had never been an elegant man. Just as she was not an elegant woman.

The first time a colleague appeared at her desk to express the appropriate regret, Elise didn't know what to say. She knew the form of words expressing sorrow was traditional, but one more it struck her as strange how so many people were apparently sorry for something that was not their fault.

As the morning wore on, she had to fight to stop smiling. She wasn't sure how people would react if she smiled at them as it wasn't what the bereaved were supposed to do. So instead, she kept on thanking people politely and indeed sincerely whilst wearing half a frown. It seemed to do the trick. Although, every now and again she couldn't help wondering how bizarre it would be if one of her colleagues had indeed had something to do with Gerald's death and was now attempting to make good the crime. It wasn't likely to be something covered by the Human Resources (HR to other staff) manual.

Perhaps she would suggest it. But not today.

Then the phone rang. Elise knew the moment she heard the voice on the other end of the line that it was going to be trouble. It was Simon, one of the more argumentative departmental deans and it was always trouble of some kind. Not that he wasn't, outside work, an averagely pleasant chap, but in work Elise always found him to be a stickler for the rules to the point of insanity. And though Elise was many things, a stickler wasn't one of them.

"Hello, Simon," she said with as much enthusiasm as possible. "How are you?"

"I'm lovely, Elise," Simon replied in his usual ebullient style. "But I'm very concerned about your handling of the Timetabling Process Review Group. Did you know you've invited one of Diana's assistant departmental deans to the rescheduled meeting as well?"

Simon paused to allow the apparent horror of her rebellious act to sink in, but frankly Elise didn't give the proverbial damn. Simon obviously hadn't heard about her recent widowhood but then again he wasn't a man who listened much to anything he himself hadn't said. More to the point, she hadn't realised that checking her list of attendees, finding that Diana had forwarded the meeting request to a member of her team, and including that person in her rescheduled meeting list was such a heinous crime. Simon had obviously never met Gerald, so had no idea what real crime looked like.

She decided to go with the soothing option, a rare decision for her. "Is that so bad?" she countered.

The response was overwhelming, or would have been if she'd paid more than a cursory attention to it.

"Is it so bad? *Is it so bad?"* Simon spat so hard down the line that Elise could almost feel the saliva hitting her ear. "If you invite one assistant department dean from one faculty, and then none of the others in the other departments, then how does that look to everyone else? It's a professional and political disaster! Everyone will think Hugh is favouring one department above the rest, so all their timetabling needs are going to be met before anyone else's. It'll be appalling for staff morale. People won't want to be bothered to do anything useful and it'll set a very nasty precedent and …"

At this point, Elise mentally switched off, let Simon rant on and began to rearrange the coloured paperclips on her desk instead. Prioritisation of urgent issues was, after all, her great skill. Usually she preferred the red ones on the left of the box and the green ones on the right, but today she thought a change might be nice. Would it set a precedent for all further paperclip-based dealings? One could only hope.

A brief silence in her ear told her Simon had stopped, or he was drawing breath for his next verbal assault, Lord preserve her. She'd better get in quickly before it all quite simply became too much to bear without being rude. She cast her mind back to the last words she'd caught before her attention strayed. Goodness, the paperclips did look nice.

"So," she said, "it'll set a very nasty precedent, the departmental deans will start a small civil war, the pro-vice chancellors will write a blog about it that nobody reads, and the vice-chancellor will have to write a letter to the paper yet again in order to calm his nerves? Goodness me, Simon, I never knew I had such powers."

"You are not taking this seriously!" This time, Simon really did start to shout and Elise had to hold the phone away from her ear until she'd grown used to the increased volume. "Hugh won't like what you've done at all, as it will cause significant problems now and into the future. First off, we need to uninvite the extra departmental staff member, and then we need to draft a new process to ensure this kind of mistake doesn't happen again. I'm going to have to discuss it with Hugh to see what can be done."

Good, Elise thought. There was nothing Hugh enjoyed more than a discussion about administrative process. Mind you, if he gave her even one iota more work than she was expecting this week, then she might well set up a two-hour meeting between him and Simon to discuss it. Maybe she did have more power than she imagined.

For now, the best way to end any argument was, she'd learnt, with a deadly mix of enthusiasm and sarcasm. It was another of her great skills. "That sounds like a wonderful idea, Simon," she said accordingly. "We'll take it under consideration for you."

Then she put the phone down. The ultimate secretarial revenge.

"What's that, Elise? Any problems?" Hugh's voice behind her sent unexpected shivers up her spine. It was odd how he was such a big man but could creep from place to place without ever making any sound. Like an elephant, but not quite as grey.

"No problems, Hugh!" she trilled in a manner fitting to a PA of a certain age, she hoped. "Everything's under control."

He smiled at her, though not with the confidence she would have liked, and padded away to some meeting or other. Yes, definitely like an elephant. A kindly one, however. He'd been such a support and indeed a revelation at Gerald's funeral. Elise wouldn't forget it.

The poor man though. These days, he had a diary stuffed full of meetings, even though Elise wasn't entirely sure such meetings ever achieved anything that couldn't be done by email or by chatting to the other person. She minuted most of the meetings herself and really they seemed to make a lot of issues far more complex than they needed to have been.

Take the meetings involving which projects were taken on by the Registry IT team and which weren't. In her six months here, it had started off simply enough, with an Operations Group which, so far, had met together twice. A quarterly meeting. Still, even though Elise had allocated two hours to sorting out what should be done when, it still hadn't managed to make any decisions. However, the Operations Group had bravely decided that there needed to be both a Group they could report to and also a sub-group which actually looked at which projects might be important.

So an Operations Governing Board had been created which included key people from the Operations Group and a few others floating around in the higher echelons of the University. It had met twice too, so far, and had simply had the same discussions as the Operations Group had had. The executive attendees had attended only once, at the beginning, and had discussed something entirely different which wasn't in the Governing Board's remit. Elise hadn't been sure what the Board was for as the minutes she'd taken had been virtually identical. It was the way the University worked, in that issues were often discussed very thoroughly indeed by various and fluctuating groups of people but few decisions were made.

Whilst all this had been going on, the sub group had also met on a two-monthly basis to look at projects people wanted to have done. Elise had found the paperwork involved in preparing for the sub-group to be so weighty as to be almost beyond her ability to carry. There were seven people in the sub-group, a few of whom Elise had never seen around before and whom she suspected might be simple passers-by on campus who'd been unlucky enough to be in the area when the sub-group attendance list was decided.

Not only did Elise have to print out seven copies of all the project bids to be discussed in the sub-group, but she also had to print out the Excel spreadsheet listing them all. In the spreadsheet, projects were divided into six categories: mandatory; important; under consideration; small projects not worth the mention; deprioritised; and done. As far as she could see, projects floated between categories on the whim of the moment and occasionally got entirely lost in the undergrowth.

Elise couldn't blame them. These days she felt a little lost in the undergrowth herself. Anyway, once four or five projects had been prioritised by the sub-group, they were then taken for approval to the Operations Group, and then for further approval to the Governing Board. The process could take weeks, and often months.

Indeed, by the time the project had final sign-off, the central IT team had nine times out of ten already done it and included it in everyone's working practices. Their reasoning was that they did the work for whichever staff member was shouting the loudest at the time, a system which had worked magnificently in all universities since universities began.

The whole thing reminded Elise of her early days as a young woman in London when she'd lived with a talented violin player who played for the London Symphony Orchestra. The violin player once remarked she didn't know why they had visiting conductors who kept encouraging them to play Mozart in a different way. When the night of the concert began, the orchestra played Mozart the way they'd always played him, whatever the conductor was doing.

The University IT project prioritisation system was very similar, to Elise's mind; whatever happened in the high-up powers, the IT staff did it the way they always had. And everything chuntered on very nicely indeed. This was the way things worked. It was the life she knew.

Still, on this first day back to the office, by the time lunchtime arrived, Elise had had enough of putting on a sorrowful face for the sole purpose of making others feel better, and decided it was time to escape to the campus lake. She bought a ham and mustard sandwich at the university shop to supplement the fruit she brought from home, and strolled to her favourite bench. It was vacant, and she couldn't help wondering if this would somehow turn out to be the best part of her day.

Settling down onto the wooden slats, Elise stretched backwards to catch the soft rays of sunshine glittering through the trees. She was wearing a jumper and fleece so she wasn't cold. When she positioned herself just so, nobody walking along the path could see her until they had almost passed by, as the bushes framing the bench were in the perfect position for secrecy. It was why she loved it the most. Sitting here in her lunch hour meant she could be truly alone, at nobody's beck and call. It gave her an essential opportunity to regroup. Dealing with people, no matter how fond of them she might be, wore her down, almost as if rodents were nibbling her away. It worried her sometimes how she might disappear entirely if she didn't allow time for herself.

Now, she simply took in the bleak sunshine and admired the calmness of the lake whilst the breeze soothed her. She could see a few people on the other side but they were far enough away not to disturb her, as she enjoyed the quiet industry of the ducks and the one or two Canada geese. Occasionally, the ducks would be eager for food, which Elise didn't give them, but they left her alone today.

Elise spent the next ten minutes working out what she was going to do with all the new information she now had about her husband. It had been churning round her mind all morning and it felt very liberating to be able to make some decisions. Ten minutes was roughly the time she always took to make any significant decisions. The insignificant decisions took longer. But Elise had always been gifted with the ability to see all the angles of any given problem very quickly and decide on a course of action. It was a large part of the reason why she was such a good secretary. Or so she told herself.

Then again, she had no reason to be smug. Because whether she could carry out her proposed course of action and whether she could get any answers were two separate aspects of the conundrum. One hurdle at a time, she told herself. One hurdle at a time.

A disturbance at her side startled her from her reverie and she almost dropped her apple. That wouldn't do. She'd been a great believer in the benefits of an apple a day from a very young age, and hadn't had any cause to change her views since. When she looked up, Hugh was gazing at her, half-smiling.

"May I sit down?" he asked. "If I'm not disturbing you, that is."

"Please do." Elise made room on the bench, though in all honesty it was a gesture only; the bench was more than long enough for several people, not just two.

Hugh folded his height down beside her and leaned forward on his knees. He looked as if he were about to come up with some ancient wisdom she would do well to listen to, but in actual fact for a good few moments he said nothing. Then again, Hugh was, like Gerald, a man of few words, so she didn't know why she'd expected anything different.

Did that make her manager, like her husband, a potential criminal? There was something to ponder on for sure. She was just casting her thoughts round for some easy topic of conversation to break the apparent impasse when Hugh surprised her entirely by getting there first.

"I wanted to talk about Gerald," he said. "I don't care whether the reports are true or not, but I wanted you to know I'm here to help, if you need me to. You've been a good employee and a great secretary to me all my years here, Elise. I hope I can count you as a friend. I certainly count you as one, though I know it's not anything I've ever said. Not directly. I'm sorry for that too. I'm not good at expressing myself when it comes to personal matters. Heaven knows, my ex was right about that. So I'm sorry if all this is very clumsy but I wanted you to know it, no matter how unEnglish it might be. Whatever you decide, Elise, I'm on your side."

She thought he might say more but when he didn't, Elise opened her mouth to reply. What she said wasn't what she assumed she would say, however.

"Thank you," she said, and reached over to put her hand on his for a moment. In that moment, he gripped her back warmly before letting go. It felt nice. "Thank you. I do appreciate that, and you. What I really wonder though is if you'll want to be on my side once I tell you what I'm planning to do about the whole Gerald scenario."

Elise paused, wondering how she'd become the kind of woman who could say the word "scenario" with some seriousness. She hoped Hugh would forgive her such a modern term; it wasn't usually her way. Still, she wouldn't think about it now. She would carry on.

"This is what I'm planning," she said. "I'm going to contact the people Gerald worked with on his illicit activities and see what they know about him. You saw them at the funeral. Really, you couldn't miss them: a youngish man with three bodyguards. As least, it's what I imagine they are as they weren't like any secretaries I've ever met. I've already got the police view of my husband, and now I want the criminal view too. I'd like to carry out my own investigations. I don't know if I'm going to find anything out about Gerald, let alone this money he's alleged to have stolen. And I don't know if I'm cut out to be an investigator. It's not a career choice I would opt for, as an ordinary woman. But I'm going to try. And I don't plan to tell the police either. This isn't for them. It's for me."

Out of breath, and out of anything else to confess, Elise stopped. She thought Hugh might object. He was, after all, a very moral man. Instead he smiled and nodded as if what she'd just admitted to him made every sense.

"I've never seen you as an ordinary woman, Elise," he said. "An extraordinary one, more like. Nothing you can say or do will change my opinion about, or my affection for, you, if that's not too intense a statement to make from your boss. What can I do to help you?"

## Chapter Eight

An interesting and heartening question. However, as it turned out, Elise had absolutely no time between going back to work and the onset of Christmas to carry out any kind of investigation. Her weeks away from the office meant she had to concentrate on dealing with the amount of paperwork – virtual and otherwise – which had been festering in her absence. Still, every so often, she found herself remembering both Hugh's loyalty and Lottie's compassion, and smiling to herself. She wasn't used to being on the receiving end of kindness from anyone but Gerald. It felt … how did it feel exactly?

It felt reassuring. Gerald had always been comforting but never reassuring. There was a difference, although Elise couldn't have fully explained it.

So, she typed and smiled, and smiled and typed, as was her wont as a secretary to a fairly important man, and soon enough the Christmas holidays came.

"I hope you have a good break," Hugh said as they were both getting ready to close down for the year. "You're having Christmas with your neighbour, you say?"

Elise nodded. When people had asked – people who weren't Lottie, that is – she'd said she was spending Christmas Day with her neighbour. The majority of enquirers had smiled with relief that they weren't honour-bound to offer her a place at their table and agreed with her what a good idea it was. Nobody wanted her to be on her own at Christmas, especially after so recently becoming a widow. Elise had nodded her agreement, though actually she was looking forward to being on her own.

She was looking forward to getting up early and paying her polite respects to the Almighty at the local cathedral. Gerald had always favoured a lie-in at Christmas, so Elise had never gone to church before on Christmas morning. Mind you, she didn't go to church at any other time – but Christmas service attendance was to do with culture, not faith. So she was looking forward to the change.

She also planned to avoid any hint of a turkey or other festive bird, and to bake herself a simple lasagne instead. It would do for a couple of days after Christmas as well. She was a great believer in eating food up, rather than throwing it away. It was an immensely satisfying act. Heavens, how proud her grandmother would have been. Elise's grandmother was the kind of woman who could take chicken bones and make from them a good wholesome soup for a family for a week. This was a great talent. For pudding – Elise was a woman who believed in *pudding* and never gave the time of day to *dessert* – she would have a mince pie, accompanied with her own home-made rum butter. The recipe was something she made each year and, even though Gerald preferred shop-bought brandy butter, she'd insisted he ate it.

It was the only thing in their married life she'd ever truly insisted on. From what she knew now, perhaps she should have insisted on more. Such as openness, honesty and some sense of ethical values – though she herself had never set much store on the latter. Too late now, and in any case every marriage had its secrets. It was how couples survived, and ultimately flourished. And Gerald had never done what to Elise was the worst crime of all – he'd never been unfaithful. As far as she knew … Hmm, perhaps when she finally met Luke and his colleagues, this was something she would have to clarify. She hoped there at least her instincts would be proved right.

So Elise made her rum butter, half-measures only so she wouldn't have too much left over, and went to bed. It was liberating not to have to decorate the house, something she and Gerald had done though on a minimum scale over the years. Not decorating any rooms for Christmas felt as if she were stepping out into something new. More than that, it was stepping out into something new which didn't involve Gerald's dubious activities. No wonder it was so welcome.

Just before slipping gently into a relatively dreamless sleep on Christmas Eve, Elise remembered her promise to confront – if confront was the right word – Luke and his gang about her husband. She would do so in the New Year. Nobody wanted to create difficulties at Christmas.

She went to sleep smiling.

In the morning, the world was deliciously quiet. Gerald had always turned on the radio as soon as he woke up, so previous Christmases had been heralded –

appropriately enough, Elise knew – with hymns and the odd festive sermon. Strange how they'd listened to hymns but never attended church together and yet this first Christmas as a widow, the radio was silent, and she was already planning when she should leave the house.

Life from now on would be different and perhaps even interesting. Elise enjoyed interesting. She only wished she'd known just how interesting Gerald would turn out to be. Typical man – happy with the concept of dull comfort but keeping his inner dangerous truths from her. She would have been more than happy to deal with them, if only he'd trusted her.

Nothing to be done about it now. So Elise bathed, dressed, had her breakfast and cleaned her teeth before setting out in very good time for the early cathedral service. 8am suited her very well. The last thing she wanted for Christmas was a church-full of children in a state of hyperactivity. If this made her a misery-guts, then so be it. She could only be what she was, and she was delightful enough in society where children weren't in attendance. What more could anyone want?

Such admittedly smug thoughts filled her mind all the way to the Cathedral and during most of the service. She thought that with what she'd been through recently she was probably entitled to smug of some description. The feeling soon limped away at the Cathedral and instead weariness replaced it.

She'd last been to a church service, admittedly not a Christmas one, when she was a young teenager. It had been the final conscious attempt she'd made to please her mother and hadn't been a great success. Strangely, all these years on, Elise felt as if nothing had changed. Something inside her had hoped the church had moved on while she'd been away, much as she had. But today's service, though different in tone and focus, was drearily similar to the one she'd experienced as a bored teenager too many years ago.

Hmm. She'd been right about God then and it was very good indeed to realise she was right about him today. He was definitely not to be relied on for excitement. As a result, Elise didn't bother with communion and instead stared at the artwork on the walls in an attempt to understand what it might be trying to say. Cathedrals these days must be trying to attract young worshippers was the only reason she could find for it. Whatever it was trying to say to her, she wasn't attuned to hear it.

When the service finally ended, Elise ran the gauntlet of smiling people trying to shake her hand whilst wishing her the compliments of the season and eventually arrived in the open air. It was raining but it still felt like escape. She certainly wouldn't be doing this again. Gerald, in his lack of enthusiasm at any kind of churchgoing, had been irritatingly right.

She would keep that realisation in the balance scales, but her dead husband still had a fair amount of ground to make up. She continued, in many ways, to reserve judgement.

Elise drove back home, hoping Lottie wouldn't spot her return. She didn't want her neighbour to think she was trying to deceive her. Of course, this was exactly what Elise was trying to do, but she would prefer Lottie didn't realise it. In Lottie's mind, Elise was already enjoying Christmas with Hugh and his extended family. And in Hugh's mind, she was enjoying the day with Lottie.

Goodness me, Elise thought. Being a widow was more complicated than she'd imagined. And she wasn't even taking into account being a criminal's widow. As long as she kept both the untruths she'd told intact, however, she would be fine. People never enquired too deeply as to her social engagements; they were simply satisfied she had some.

Not having them was even better. In the kitchen, she was congratulating herself how well she'd done in her new career of deception – though perhaps not as well as Gerald – when the doorbell rang.

Elise groaned, but quietly. She'd just opened the kitchen window to let some air in, and she didn't want whoever it was to realise her lack of enthusiasm for visitors. It was bound to be Lottie, wasn't it? She'd been spotted – and her reputation in the road was already noted as being anti-social, so perhaps she should have groaned more loudly. Lottie – or whoever it was – might have gone away.

She cast one longing look at the kettle and her solitary and favourite mug nestling by it before squaring her shoulders and heading to the door.

The shape through the frosted glass was distinctly taller than Lottie's petite form. When Elise opened up, she saw it was, of all people, Hugh.

"Hello," he launched into an introduction before she could even think about welcoming him. "I know you weren't expecting me, but I wasn't convinced you were telling the truth about your Christmas plans. I thought about ringing you but I knew I wouldn't get the truth then either. So the only option was to visit you, as you can see. So, happy Christmas, Elise. Are you really spending it with your neighbour?"

To her surprise, Elise began to laugh. It somehow didn't matter Hugh had unmasked her innocent deceit. Especially not when compared to Gerald's far greater crimes. A white lie or two was surely nothing when set against fraud. She stepped aside and waved Hugh into the hallway. "Happy Christmas to you too. And, no, I'm not spending the day with Lottie, my neighbour that is. Then again, you're not the only one I've lied to. I told Lottie I was spending it with you."

As Hugh took off his jacket, he shook his head in mock despair. "And there was I thinking I was the only one you'd tried to deceive. Though, come to think of it, you're spending at least some of the day with me, so you've inadvertently told Lottie the truth."

"Oh good, I really couldn't have borne the guilt otherwise."

Elise took Hugh's jacket and hung it up in the coat cupboard before ushering him through to the living room. He sat down on one of the individual armchairs, not the right hand section of the two-seater sofa, which had been Gerald's domain. His choice heartened her. "Tea? Coffee?"

Hugh opted for coffee, as she'd thought he would though it was always polite to ask. You really knew with men. Gerald had always been a coffee drinker at home though whilst on holiday abroad he'd invariably chosen tea. On a couple of occasions in their early married life, Elise had teased him about it and offered him tea on their return home. His response had been to stare at her in amazement. Apparently, tea was for holidays, and coffee was for normal domestic life. He'd always been an odd man. She wondered now, as she boiled the kettle for Hugh, if Gerald drank tea or coffee with his criminal friends. When she met them, she would be sure to ask.

Something else occurred to her as she poured her visitor a cup and found some distinctly unseasonal digestive biscuits to add to a tray. Did he expect lunch and, if so, what sort? She would, as her grandmother used to say, have him asked and soon.

"What about you?" Elise asked as she deposited the tray on the coffee table. Thankfully Hugh had cleared a space. Which reminded her she ought to do a tidy-up at some point though, with Gerald and his neatness obsession gone, what would be the point? "Weren't you supposed to be at your cousin's house today? Or were you lying about your whereabouts as well?"

"Sadly not," Hugh replied, clutching his mug in both hands and leaning forward in contemplative pose. "I might have been better off if I'd gone to ground, like you have. I arrived at my cousin Barry's at 9.30 this morning, as promised, where I found him in the middle of a huge row with Jan, his wife, about the nanny. Apparently, he's been having an affair with the nanny for the last six months, and Jan found out about it yesterday. Suffice it to say she's not best pleased and was sharing her opinions with him and most of the street too. In the general horror of it, they forgot all about me so I thought it was best to make a strategic withdrawal before Barry decided to ask me to pick a side. Because, if it's true and I have to say it does appear to be, I would obviously be on Jan's side. I mean how do people have the time to have affairs? They must be a lot more organised than I am."

"Or have very organised secretaries willing to turn a blind eye," Elise suggested with a sympathetic smile. "I'm sorry to hear it though. Haven't they been married for years?"

Hugh sighed and took a sip of his coffee. "Fifteen years. And they lived together a while before that. Mind you, with the revelations Jan was sharing with everyone this morning about Barry, it's clear I've never really known him at all. You never can tell, can you?"

With that he coughed and turned bright red. "Sorry. That was crass."

Elise shook her head. "Don't worry about it. I've heard worse. But you're right. You never can tell."

They were both silent for a few moments. Elise breathed in the delicious and comforting scent of coffee filling the living room and thought about Gerald. Honestly, she could have sworn she thought about him more often now he was dead than she ever had when he was alive. Perhaps this was the essence of a successful marriage; instinct and acceptance rather than thought were the bywords.

She couldn't tell what Hugh was thinking about – which was in many ways the essence of a successful friendship and a good relationship with one's boss. She did need to clear something up first, however. "Hugh?"

"Yes?" he turned again towards her, the flush on his skin easing now.

"I think if you, of all people, are going to react with such sensitivity to every innocent comment which might – or might not – remind me of Gerald, then any conversation is going to take a long time to reach a conclusion. Why not just agree to let things go? If I feel offended at any point, I'll be sure to let you know directly, without you having to second-guess me. After all, it's what I usually do at work, isn't it?"

Hugh grinned at that. "It certainly is. It's a deal then, Elise."

He stretched out his hand and Elise took it. Her fingers felt lost in his, but his skin felt warm and comforting. Like the smell of coffee or arrival home after a long journey. It felt like a promise and a beginning, though why this should be so was a mystery.

"Agreed," she said as he let her go. "And thank you."

In the end, Hugh stayed until almost 4pm, when the light was definitely beginning to fade. For lunch, the two of them made a simple tuna pasta bake together, Hugh helping out in the kitchen without making any unnecessary fuss. There, Elise thought, was the difference between a married and a divorced man; the latter was well able to understand the ebb and flow of kitchen etiquette whereas, for the former – in her experience –it was a mystery. The very fact that the day eschewed the concept of anything remotely Christmassy was a delight. Never had tuna and pasta tasted so good or been so magnificently finished off with a portion of plain yoghurt and Greek honey.

The glass or two of Champagne only made it all the more delicious.

Elise was just considering whether it would be discourteous to her visitor to switch on the repeat of the Queen's Speech when the doorbell interrupted her for the second time today. Goodness, she'd never been this popular since her last birthday when she'd bought cakes for the office.

This time it was Lottie. Ah, she'd been spotted then. Elise decided to brazen it out and all the more as she didn't want her kind neighbour to think ill of her.

"Lottie! How lovely to see you. Please come in. Happy Christmas!"

"Happy Christmas to you too," Lottie replied before giving Elise another unexpected hug. Though whether they should be less unexpected now she knew Lottie better would be something Elise would need to consider further. "I thought you were away, but I saw your car earlier on and thought you might like this."

From nowhere, Lottie produced a plant that was almost half her size and a box of chocolates which would have kept the whole Roman army well fed for a week. Yes, perhaps Elise exaggerated the size of the offerings but the social trauma of receiving presents from people not in her virtually non-existent present-buying circle had coloured her view.

"That's really too kind of you," she said, and meant it too. "Thank you so much. Would you like tea?"

"I'd love a cup," her neighbour replied. "And, just so you know, the plant's a bromeliad. It doesn't need much water so if you make sure the little cup shape at its centre is fairly full, and refill it every now and again, it should be fine."

A bromeliad. Elise hadn't heard of such a plant before but, as she took a closer look at it, she couldn't help but admire the shape. It was a tall, spiky plant with a flurry of green leaves at the bottom and purple striped spindles at the top. Somehow, of all the plants in all the world that Lottie could have chosen, Elise felt it was likely to be the most suitable one for her.

Both women leaned over it to stare at the cup shape in the middle. It was indeed full of water. What an excellent system of irrigation. Elise smiled at Lottie and thanked the woman again. This time she meant it more fulsomely.

Before switching on the kettle, she took her neighbour through to the living room to meet Hugh. Her boss was already standing up near the door, with that particular smile on his face he used to greet visitors he wasn't sure about. It made Elise smile too – she knew it so well.

"This is Hugh," she explained to Lottie. "He's my boss. Hugh – this is Lottie, my neighbour. Of course you met at the funeral."

"Yes, we did." Lottie shook Hugh's outstretched hand. "Elise said she'd be spending Christmas with you, but I hadn't realised you'd be here."

Hugh nodded. "Last minute change of plan, I'm afraid. I suspected Elise's house would be in a better state than my own and I was right. Lovely to meet you again, Lottie, and a happy Christmas to you."

After Elise fetched tea and refreshed her own and Hugh's coffees, the three of them sat down. Elise thought it would definitely be incorrect to watch the Queen's speech now. It was worse to be socially rude to two people than it was to simply one.

"How're the family?" she asked Lottie, a sudden flash of her previous, brief chats about the Christmas season coming to mind at last. "You have the children staying, don't you?"

This was more than enough of a prompt to get Lottie onto her favourite subject. Elise wasn't greatly fond of children herself, but she was always happy to meet people who did have them and loved it. There was something about the joy of other people fulfilled which gave her hope for her own life, although in an entirely different arena.

Did that mean she'd been dissatisfied with Gerald and had been given new hope now? She didn't think it was quite so simple and would vehemently have defended herself against any such accusations in public. Still, her own reactions were making her think, while she listened to her neighbour's brief run-down of what the children were up to.

Lottie had two children, both in their twenties. Richard was an up-and-coming actor and had had walk-on parts in a smattering of crime dramas, some of which Elise had seen. The amount of lines he was given was gradually increasing, which could only be a good thing.

Lottie's daughter, Susan, was more down-to-earth, and now Elise thought of it, she could remember having rather a good conversation with Susan at one of Lottie's recent parties. This year, she'd just started up her own business designing websites and helping companies with publicity, and she appeared to be doing well. Elise had been impressed with Susan's modesty and couldn't help warming to her. She thought both Lottie's children were a credit to her and said so.

Lottie glowed with evident pride at Elise's words. "I'm not sure how much it has to do with me. I don't think I can take any credit for it though of course, like any proud mother, I can't help basking in the reflected glory."

Hugh laughed, but Elise felt moved to disagree. "There's no harm in basking at all. I strongly suspect you're entitled to it. Gerald and I never had children – we never wanted to – but I imagine if we had, they'd never be half as motivated as your two. Goodness, they might even have turned to a criminal life, as my husband appears to have done, and then heaven only knows what would have happened. I may well be a gangster's wife, though I hope in the Surrey rather than the American style, but I don't think I would have wanted to found a gangster dynasty. Not without being fully aware of it, that is."

Perhaps she shouldn't have been so direct? A quick glance at Lottie showed her that her neighbour was possibly casting about for a suitable neighbourly answer to Elise's honesty. However, it was Hugh who smoothed the path.

"On the other hand," he chipped in just as Lottie opened her mouth, "on the other hand, a gangster dynasty might well be the only way of getting things done at the university. All those committees we have to attend just slow everything down."

Elise blinked at him, and then all three of them began to laugh. She'd never heard her boss express anything quite so radical and had always believed him to be a dedicated company man through and through. So much for her opinion and judgements. She evidently had no idea about how to read the characters of the men she knew. She was going to have to pay more attention in the future.

Then again, there were several things that were going to be different in the future, she thought later on that afternoon when both her visitors had departed.

Starting with a long chat with Gerald's colleague Luke at some point very soon.

## Chapter Nine

The first day back at work after Christmas could always go one way or the other, to Elise's mind. This year Hugh was away for another week so she had time to gain some kind of control over the action-packed life of the Registry before he returned. She wanted him to be impressed with her industry. She actually did always feel that way, as she liked Hugh very much and thought he had quite a rough deal at the university. This time, however, it felt even more important that he was in some way impressed, and she couldn't really understand why. Funny, that.

The good thing was it was a Thursday, and Thursdays she only worked in the morning. After 1pm today and until 9am on Monday, Elise's time was her own.

Today, what with experiencing her first Christmas as a widow, it had completely slipped her mind that one of her colleagues, Amy, would be returning after maternity leave. It was Elise's responsibility, as the Registry secretary, to arrange computer and phone connections. She'd been trying to organise it early in December but

Gerald had died and then everything had changed. So, she would need to do it today, for certain. Beyond ensuring Amy's connections were working, Elise's plan was to leave at 1pm, come what might, and escape in the direction of the shops.

On her desk, Elise was less than delighted to find a generic New Year gift from the University which consisted of (a) a CD-size calendar for the year ahead showcasing suitable pictures of the campus and its star students; and (b) a copy of the monthly University review, which Elise made a point of never reading.

Really, she would have preferred a bottle of good white wine and a small box of Lindor chocolates, but she supposed it was out of the question.

"Holiday okay?" One of her colleagues, Jack, lifted his eyebrows at her from opposite her desk. Elise had never known a time when she was in before him and sometimes she wondered if he ever went home at all.

"Yes, thanks, not bad under the circumstances. You?"

"Could have done without the three day cold, but at least it kept me off turkey duty for a while."

Elise laughed. After the ups and downs (really, more downs than ups) of last month, being able to laugh felt very good indeed. She and Jack chatted for a while about Christmas, weather and family. For the latter subject, he talked and she listened, as she didn't have any family to talk about. Not any more.

When Amy arrived, with her manager Karen, it reminded Elise of what needed to be done. So far this morning, no computer and no phone connection man had appeared.

So, it was up to her to leap into action of some kind, if a woman of her age still had the capacity to leap. Elise hoped she did. Indeed she would go so far as to say she assumed it. She liked to think she continued to have the capacity to do a great many things, whether or not they included Gerald.

While Amy and Karen began to bring the files over from Amy's old office, Elise rang IT to see what time they were going to connect her colleague. The unfortunate man at the other end of the line obviously had no idea what Elise was talking about.

"Didn't you get my email three weeks ago with the completed form you asked for?"

"Yes," was the jaded reply. "But that job reference has been closed off. We thought it had been finished."

"Oh. Please could it be reinstated, so Amy can get to work on the computer? She's been away on maternity leave for ten months, so there'll be six thousand emails needing attention."

"At least!" the computer man said with a laugh. "Don't worry, I'll send someone down. There's not much else to do at the moment."

Well, thank goodness for that, Elise thought. This was her first attempt at getting someone's desk arranged for them since the lady who used to do it had moved departments. It wouldn't look good if it was a complete disaster from the start. People had long memories about failure in the university world, though perhaps having a dead, allegedly criminal husband might give her some kind of leeway. You never knew. There had to be a plus side to the revelations about Gerald, didn't there?

By the time Amy and Karen returned, pushing a trolley full of folders that made Elise wonder about the relevance of the paperless office, the IT men were already on the case. In a manner of speaking. They were both kneeling under Amy's new desk, staring at the set of plugs they found.

"Any luck?" Karen asked, and Elise shook her head.

"Still working on it, I'm afraid. The phone might be all right though."

"Damn it," Amy said. "Really, if it's a problem, I'm happy without the phone. I'd take the computer over the phone any day."

Elise could only agree, in a work setting anyway. Now of course would be the perfect moment to ask Amy about her new daughter, but for the life of her Elise couldn't remember the child's name. Even though she was sure Karen had told her at least five times. Elise wasn't a fan of children and tried to avoid them at all costs but even she knew asking about the daughter would be the decent thing to do.

If only she could remember the name.

After a couple of seconds which were tense – though probably only to Elise – she fudged it.

"Happy new year, Amy," she said with a bright smile. "And welcome back to the office."

It seemed to be enough and for the next few minutes, while the IT team continued to struggle away under the desks with whatever strange magic they were performing, the three women caught up on their respective Christmases. In a very short amount of time, Elise found out that Karen, her partner Sarah and their four cats had survived a series of power cuts relatively well, thanks to LED lighting and a camping stove, though there'd been a dodgy moment or two with Sarah's frail parents but it hadn't been as bad as the war years, according to them. Amy and the family, on the other hand, had spent Christmas with her in-laws and a sick child. Not the ideal combination.

Elise was about to give up waiting to hear what Amy's child was called when Amy herself laid a hand on her arm.

"I'm sorry about Gerald," she said. "I didn't know whether to write you a note or not, but then I didn't know your address and I knew I'd see you when I came back to work. So I just wanted to say I was sorry about it."

"Thank you," Elise said and patted Amy's hand. "It means a lot."

It did too. From nowhere, Amy's simple words spoke to Elise in a way which all the stumbled though heartfelt commiserations she'd received at the office after Gerald's death had not. Perhaps it was progress in whatever the grieving process was supposed to be? In any case, Elise wished she had half Amy's sense of graciousness. Something to aim for in the year of her widowhood then.

It didn't take Elise long to catch up with her emails. Certainly not as long as it took the IT men to plug in Amy's computer, unplug it again, search for a longer cable which didn't affect anyone else, and replug the computer, this time with success. There then followed an hour of working out what to do with the phone, including the suggestion of a new handset or a phone expert to take a long hard look at the problem.

At that point, Amy's telephone rang and everyone jumped and stared at it. Elise felt a wave of hysteria rising in her throat but thought she ought to push it back down for the sake of sanity. Her own and everyone else's. She was sure if she started to laugh on this most difficult of days, she wouldn't be able to stop. That way, as Shakespeare put it, madness lies.

"That'll be the phone," said Karen. A statement which was undeniable. "Maybe you should answer it."

Amy did. There was a few moments' conversation with what appeared to be another IT man on the other end of the line and then she replaced the receiver. "The phone's working. They don't really know why but it is."

"It's because we're so good at our jobs," said the older of the two IT men as they crawled out from under Amy's desk. "Even we can't explain it."

It was only after they'd gone and the office had settled down again that Amy glanced at her phone. "Damn. I didn't think to ask them what my new number is. Still, the fewer people know, the better."

There was truth there, Elise thought.

The morning stumbled on in the way that mornings at work tended to do, but Elise was entirely up to date with everything by the time 1pm finally arrived.

The first Thursday afternoon back after work in January was always the one day in the year Elise ventured to the sales, and also tended to be one of the few days in the year she went shopping at all. She wasn't a great fan of shopping, in spite of her gender. In fact, she'd often wondered if she'd missed the lesson at secondary school about How to Be A Girl through illness. It wouldn't surprise her, though it didn't bother her and Gerald had never complained.

Then again, he'd had more exciting things on his mind, hadn't he? Elise never wearing a skirt in her adult life hadn't been high up on Gerald's list of problems. Goodness, she should stop thinking like this and simply go and do the shopping she needed. Then, tomorrow on her day off, she would visit Luke and his gang. She'd seen his address in one of the police files during her visit to the station.

Feeling more adventurous than she'd anticipated, Elise signed off for the week and drove into town. The road was quieter than she'd feared, which was only a positive thing. Elise wasn't a fan of big crowds. Finding a parking space was simple enough and Elise made her way through the underpass and across the small private car park to the bottom of the High Street. The underpass was dotted with water, and she wondered if it had flooded in the recent weather conditions. It was passable enough now. As she crossed the bridge, the water level did indeed look higher than usual to her untrained eye. She'd best get the goods she'd come in for and make her escape from the town before high tide at 3pm.

Her usual plan was to sort out exactly the items she needed before arriving at the shops, and then sail through said shops as quickly as possible, getting only the goods she wanted. Her ideal amount of time spent in any clothes shop was five minutes. After this, she tended to get bored and irritated by the knowledge that nothing ever suited her, and the shop which stocked items Elise would like had not yet been invented.

In her youth, in the heady days of the late teens and early twenties, Elise had taken some pleasure from shopping, but it wasn't a memory she revisited often. She remembered a chain, long since defunct, called Richard Shops where she could rely on finding items she liked. If only she'd known then how such shopping ease would never come to her life again, Elise would have treasured her outings to this chain more thoroughly. However, the ability to see in to the future had not yet been discovered, not even by the Higgs-Boson team, and so she'd been doomed to remain ignorant.

She made her way up the cobbled High Street, ignoring Debenhams. She'd try there as a last resort on her way back to the car. For now, it was Marks and Spencer or nothing. Her mission: new flat shoes (her work shoes were always flat) and new nightwear. Both items felt like marking a point between who she'd been with Gerald and who she was now. A counsellor would no doubt have a lot to say about it, but Elise had no intention of speaking to any counsellor about matters which were essentially private. She never had and she never would.

It was at least a couple of years since Elise had been in Marks and Spencer with any degree of enthusiasm or commitment, and she was surprised to find the shoe department had expanded. Whether this made her desire to find a suitable pair of shoes and escape as quickly as possible easier or harder was impossible to tell on a first walk round the appropriate shelves: size seven and wide fitting. Her feet weren't her best features and never had been. For this, she blamed her mother.

A rather fancy purple pair, relatively flat, caught her eye. They weren't black, but surely still worth a look. However, when she tried them on, her bunions objected at once, which boded badly for anything beyond the demands of a few steps here and there. A shame, as the shoes were interesting.

She looked round the displays again, feeling the tug of anxiety due to the very nature of shopping pulling at her skin, bringing with it the desire to give up and be gone. Then, just as she thought she would leave, she saw a stylish pair of black flats at the corner of a shelf. Size seven and blissfully wide-fitting, it was a New Year miracle in the flesh. Elise tried them on, knew they were the ones at once, and bought them within minutes. They were far more modern than her current pair, and Rome after all had never been built in a day. She'd save the concept of colours other than black to her next shoe outing, next year.

Surely Gerald would never have coped with the thought of her changing. Or then again, seeing as she'd obviously not known him well at all, perhaps he would have been pleased. Who could say? Certainly not herself.

Feeling as if she could seriously have punched Gerald if he'd unexpectedly appeared in front of her – though what the managers of Marks and Spencer would say at such an act was unthinkable – Elise paced swiftly to the escalator in search of night attire on the first floor. The place was full of men returning unwanted lingerie, and women looking for something more suitable in the sales.

Elise thanked God Gerald had never been so foolish as to attempt to buy her lingerie. They hadn't had that kind of relationship and she was glad of it. If she wanted underwear she bought it herself, and he never commented. Sensible man.

She planned to ignore lingerie and head straight for nightwear, but her eye was taken with a display of non-wired bras, which included her size, astonishingly. As a 38A, Elise wasn't used to finding her size easily which was something of a nuisance. Why couldn't shopkeepers acknowledge the existence of a tall, broad-backed yet small-bosomed woman? It was a true mystery. Today, after the initial surprise, Elise found nothing she liked was in the sales which rather took the shine off her hope. Moreover, there was obviously a current glut of lace in the bra manufacturing world, but too much lace made her feel frivolous, and she wasn't a frivolous woman.

So she made her way to night attire. She could usually rely on Marks and Spencer to have something available for the woman between the ages of young and old but today her search took longer. This year, nighties were evidently being worn short, by young women who couldn't get enough silly romantic cartoons, or cute-looking dogs. Elise wasn't fond of dogs, though she could tolerate the odd cat, every now and again.

In the end, she chose a long light-blue night-gown with a subtle decoration of embroidered flowers at the neckline, and a shorter white nightie with small stars. They were the best of an uninspiring choice.

Armed with shoes and night-attire, Elise wandered through the handbag section but found nothing to her liking. She'd been hoping to get everything done in one shop and then escape to the relative sanity of home, but it was not to be.

Goods paid for and back out into the chill clarity of the High Street, Elise sighed and turned her attention to the House of Fraser. In her younger days, when newly married to Gerald, Elise had shopped here fairly regularly though then it had been called the Army & Navy stores. She'd liked it better before it tried to be something it wasn't. Really, the same could be said of some people too. Elise had quite a list of those.

As usual, the House of Fraser was full of young and stylish women of the type Elise had never been. The handbags were the size of postage stamps and those that were just about large enough to put a glasses case and a purse into were well over the £500 marker.

Ridiculous! Elise would rather struggle on with her old, worn out handbag than pay such a large amount of money. She gave up and turned her steps to Debenhams at the bottom of the High Street. It was on her way back to the car, so she had nothing to lose.

In Debenhams, there were shelves and shelves of handbags. More handbags than any reasonable woman could possibly use in one lifetime. Elise, deciding she was desperate to have some kind of success in her search, spent some time examining each potential buy. Half an hour later, she decided on a fairly large black leather bag with handles and a shoulder strap. She liked to cover all eventualities if she could. It was priced at £99, a figure Elise would never have paid in several lifetimes, but marked down in the sale to £69, so honour was in a small measure satisfied.

Bag paid for and job done, Elise left the store, walking out into the afternoon winter gloom, and made her way back across the car park to the underpass. At the bottom of the stairs, she was about to step smartly and confidently in the manner of all lone women everywhere through the tunnel when she realised it was full of water.

The river must be at high tide. She turned round to take the long way back to the car and it was at this precise moment that somebody grabbed her elbow and propelled her into the shadow of the stairs.

Quick as a shaft of light on a noontide shadow, Elise feinted to one side and gave her would-be assailant a good, strong kick in the unmentionables. It was a move her mother had taught her at a very young age, and Elise had never had cause to regret the lesson. The man groaned and doubled up, and Elise took the opportunity to push him down against the wall, using the largest of her shopping bags.

"Just what on earth are you up to? Don't you think I'm an easy target because I'm not. If you're planning to mug me, young man, you'd better think again."

The man coughed and looked up, his forehead crinkled into a frown. Elise gave a snort of disbelief and stepped back. She recognised his face. It was the younger of the two men who'd accompanied Luke to Gerald's funeral. Why was he attacking her?

"What do you want?" she asked again, more than ready to add a kick from one firm foot if she needed to.

The man shook his head. "I'm not a mugger. None of us would hurt the boss's family. Why would you think that? We only want to talk with you."

Ah. An interesting way of contacting her but perhaps Elise could do today what she'd planned to put off until tomorrow. Talking wasn't an activity she objected to.

## Chapter Ten

As a result, Elise decided to agree to follow her
companion, who turned out to be Hank, rather than Flank.
Elise wondered how Luke told them apart at all. In any
case, it took Hank a while to understand that, no, she had
no intention of getting into his car, but yes she was more
than happy to trundle along after him in hers. Elise
believed one of the cornerstones of female independence
was the ownership of a car, and she wasn't prepared to let
her privileges go.

Mind you, she couldn't help being envious of
Hank's car which was sleek and grey and in a far higher
price bracket than her own. Crime paid, evidently. Where
on earth had Gerald hidden that lost money?

Hank's journey took them out of town onto the A3
and towards Elise's home village. Was she being taken to
the Great Criminal Headquarters (the addition of capital
letters in her thought process was instinctive) and where
might they be? In the event, Hank turned off towards the
small town of Godalming before they reached the exit to

Elise's home. They twisted and turned their way down the long slow hill past Charterhouse and took a sharp turn right at the bottom into one of the more upmarket roads in the area.

1930s-style houses gave way to great Victorian buildings divided up into flats in the latter part of the twentieth century on the right. On the left, the houses were more modern, with ugly garages positioned in front so that the houses lurked behind like shy guests at a party. Elise fully expected she and her escort would need to find somewhere to park on the right where no garages existed, but in front of her Hank swung suddenly to the left just before the road – a cul-de-sac which dwindled to a small path into woods – ended.

She came to an abrupt halt behind him, barely missing his bumper. Didn't these people know how to use an indicator? What did they imagine it was for? Hank leapt out of his top-of-the-range vehicle and came to stand like a guard outside her door. If he was trying to stop her escaping, it was the wrong time to do it. She could have veered off course any time between the town and where they were now.

Hank evidently wasn't a man who liked to think things through. Elise pushed her door against his stomach to give her enough room to get out of her car. She wasn't particularly gentle about it, but he made no comment. He merely reddened further than he had already and stepped smartly backwards. Elise nodded her thanks.

"This way, is it?" she said as she locked the car and swept down the driveway towards the front door.

A muffled shout from Hank behind her but Elise was already at the entrance. Without waiting for her companion, she rapped on the wood, pushed open the door and stepped inside. It would of course have been normal etiquette to ring the bell and wait for a response but, by now, Elise had had enough of normal etiquette and was keen to see the effect of doing something surprising. Occasionally, it was rather exciting to shake things up a little.

"Good afternoon," she trilled in her poshest voice. "You wanted to see me and now I'm here. Anyone at home?"

The next moment, two solid individuals stood in front of her, baring her way. In the unlit hall shadows punctuated only by light from adjoining rooms, Elise could make out one man and one woman. She assumed it would be Janet and Flank, Hank being behind her.

"Hello," she said again. "You asked me to come."

Behind her, the door slammed shut, and the light came on. Interesting. Was that a feature or had Hank just had the wherewithal to press the switch? Now Elise could see more clearly, she could also see the guns the bodyguards were carrying at their waists. They made no effort to hide them. Goodness, was it legal? A moment later, the stupidity of her question made her shake her head.

"Stay right where you are, Mrs. Walker," Janet said, her voice tribute to the effect of cigarettes over many a year. In the harsh light, Elise could see the lines on the woman's face.

"I'm not moving," Elise replied. "You have the gun. But I have to say it's certainly not how Gerald or I would ever have greeted a visitor. If he were still alive, I'm sure he'd have something to say."

"Sorry!" Hank's voice chimed up from behind her. "Mrs. Walker's pretty nippy when she decides to move."

"Hank!" Elise swung round, setting to one side her promise not to move, and gave the man an accusing stare. "I'm here in front of you. You don't have to talk about me as if I'm absent. It's not polite."

He blushed again and shuffled to one side, head lowered. "Sorry," he said again.

"Mrs. W.," Janet said. "I apologise if my behaviour isn't to your liking, but both your husband and our new boss always want their bodyguards to be prepared. Now, please turn round."

Elise did so, but she was bristling, angry words crowding her throat. She couldn't help but let some of them escape. "The name's Mrs. Walker, not Mrs. W. And I'm not carrying any weapons, so your search is pointless."

Pointless, but apparently necessary. Janet said nothing else as she frisked Elise in a thorough but efficient manner. Elise half wondered if someone might suddenly leap out of a dark corner and yell 'Surprise!' But they didn't, though the experience still felt distinctly surreal.

When the frisking was done, and nothing threatening found apart from a throat sweet long past its sell-by date, Janet tapped Elise on the arm and gestured towards a door on the left. "The boss will see you now, Mrs. W… Walker."

Elise nodded. "Thank you, Janet."

Without any more ado, Elise stepped up sharply to the door indicated and marched inside. She was so through with knocking, as the young people used to say, when such a phrase was in vogue.

The moment she swung open the door and walked inside, she gasped. Everything around her was white. Tastefully and simply white, although with a subtle emptiness at its heart as if it was a blank canvas waiting for inspiration.

Luke had been sitting in a totally white armchair when she opened the door, but stood up at once as she entered the room. It was lucky he did: he was wearing a white shirt and pale trousers, so Elise might not have spotted him if he hadn't moved.

"Ah, Mrs. Walker," he said. "It's a pleasure to meet you again. Welcome to our headquarters."

"Thank you," Elise blinked to try to adjust her perspective. She'd expected something more … vibrant and criminally-inclined. Because she couldn't help it, she added, "Is this your usual choice of décor?"

Luke laughed. "Gerald always said you took no prisoners. It's nice to see my expectations being met."

Elise wasn't sure she liked the idea of her husband talking about her to these people, but she was here to discover more about his secret life and the past she never knew. She would simply have to bear it.

"You're lucky," she replied, still staring round the room and trying to take it all in. "Because, until recently, I never had any expectations at all, as I didn't know any of you existed."

Luke walked towards Elise with his hand outstretched. She took it. Politeness cost nothing.

"I'm sorry you never knew about us," he said. "I would have favoured talking with you, but Gerald was always against it. He felt you would have judged him."

Elise blinked. Her husband might have been right, though she was sorry for it. She would have judged him in some fashion or other. It hadn't been in her plan to marry a criminal, and it was perhaps therefore a good thing in many ways she hadn't known about it until after Gerald's death. If she'd discovered the truth when he was alive, she wouldn't have been able to keep her opinions to herself. Gerald hadn't been altogether fond of her opinions, particularly when fearsomely expressed.

Meanwhile, Luke waved Elise into another dazzlingly white chair next to his own before resuming his seat again. The bodyguards, Hank, Flank and Janet, ranged behind them. Elise wondered what might happen if she did something unexpected, and then decided against it.

When he sat down, Luke continued to talk, suddenly returning to her previous question about interior design.

"White is the colour of the soul," he said, though Elise wasn't sure if she believed in any kind of a soul. She wasn't a metaphysical woman. "It cleanses the mind and enables me to be the best kind of man I can be. The best kind of criminal too, which your husband appreciated very much. I like to think I was someone Gerald could rely on. He knew I was odd, but oddity can be a valuable thing and he never complained about my need for a white room. So, the reason, Mrs. Walker, that I keep my room so white is to remember and revel in the harshness and purity of life. For me it puts everything in perspective."

"Oh good," Elise said when Luke paused for breath. "I've never met a philosopher criminal before. It's most refreshing."

Luke smiled. "Why, thank you. I've never thought of it like that, but you may well be right. But forgive me, I've been remiss in my hospitality. Can I offer you a drink of some kind? Coffee? Tea?"

"Water would be lovely, thank you."

Hank sprang into action. With surprising grace, the bodyguard took a bottle of water from a cupboard she hadn't yet seen and poured half a glass from an impressive distance before handing it to Elise with a definite flourish.

"Thank you," she said. "Nicely done, I must say."

Hank smiled and leaned towards her. "I used to work as a barman. I still keep the skills up."

Elise nodded. She wasn't sure when a hired thug would need bar skills, but talent should never go unnoticed. "Good for you."

She sipped the water and settled more comfortably in her chair. Apart from the singular choice of colour, the room in which Luke got in touch with his inner soul was actually quite plush. Here was a word Elise hadn't thought of since her grandmother had died over twenty-five years ago, but it was a word that fitted.

The chairs they were sitting in were white, and Elise could see a white sofa at the edge of one white wall. Next to it was a table and a floor lamp in art deco style. All pale colours of course. To the right of this was a picture window which, as far as she could tell, looked out onto the garden. At the moment, the curtains were drawn.

Never mind, because on the other side of the wall, to Elise's left, stood a bookcase which stretched from one edge of the room to the other, and from floor to ceiling. It too was white (of course), although the books were whichever colour the publishers had opted for.

She put down her water glass. "You have a great deal of books here. Are they real or just for show?"

An unmistakeable gasp of horror from the bodyguards echoed round the room. Luke tutted loudly. "Gerald was a man of great taste," he said. "He would never have a book, or indeed anything, in his house or business premises which was just for show. Surely you know that, Mrs. Walker?"

She did too. Gerald had possessed nothing in his precious library that he hadn't either read or intended to read. "Yes, of course. But this is your room, not Gerald's."

"The house is Gerald's, though he was good enough to offer this room up to my own particular way of living. I'm not a great reader myself, I'm sorry to say. It was a source of concern to your husband. That's why the bookshelves are here. Every time your husband finished reading a book he thought I might be persuaded to open and at least leaf through, he would place it in the case for me. He was always a very considerate man."

Elise laughed. "And have you read them?"

Behind her Janet stifled what might have been a snort, but it was subtly done. Not loud enough for the mysterious, white-obsessed Luke to hear. "Oh no," he said. "I don't read. But, still, he tried and it was a very caring action."

All this was very interesting, but Elise was keen to get to the point of her visit.

"So, tell me, why exactly do you wish to speak with me?" she asked him.

Luke raised one beautifully-shaped eyebrow at her. "Isn't it obvious? We hope you can tell us where your husband hid the money," he said.

## Chapter Eleven

It wasn't every day Elise was asked to give up the illicit proceeds of crime to a dubious gang, especially those she didn't have, but she was happy to remember she'd taken it in her stride.

In any case she'd expected Luke to ask her such a question, and it was the very reason for her arrival at his home. At the time, Elise had nodded, put down her drink, surprised her hands didn't tremble, and then said – quite calmly and truthfully – that she didn't know anything and in fact she too was looking for the money. She hadn't mentioned Gerald's cryptic note, which made her feel happier. She wasn't admitting anything to the police, but neither was she giving the local mafia – if that was the right phrase – any undue advantage.

She'd always appreciated the need to play fair. And if anyone was going to come out of the encroaching mess smelling of the proverbial roses, then it was definitely going to be her.

Further conversation had ensued, though she couldn't remember the purport of any of it now, two days later. She'd been worried they might threaten her or even hold her prisoner and torture her by pulling out her nails.

She shouldn't have been so ridiculous. This was white-collar crime (in Luke's case, literally) and it wasn't the city. Anyway, she didn't have decent nails as she could never be bothered with them, so no doubt there was not enough there to pull out. Besides, Luke had in fact been even politer than the police had been, and had requested, very courteously, that she keep him informed of any developments. Really, the way he'd put it sounded more police-like than the police themselves.

When she'd left the gang headquarters – though it was probably not how they referred to it themselves - Elise could barely remember driving home, parking the car and sitting in the kitchen.

Once there, she'd started to laugh and found she couldn't stop. Not that she could blame herself. The whole thing was ridiculous. What on earth made them think a woman in her early fifties whose criminal record amounted to one parking ticket and a speeding fine – now spent –

would know anything at all about what Gerald had done with the wretched money? She had never been any kind of Bonnie to Gerald's Clyde. Not that he'd been a Clyde on any level, at least not to her.

She was still finding it hard to believe all this wasn't some kind of elaborate set-up. But it was true enough. The police, and now the gang, had been more than convincing. Elise only hoped they wouldn't find any weak links in the walls Gerald had build around them which would enable them to take away her house. It would be the final straw and she was certain she wouldn't be able to cope.

This realisation made her laugh again. Here she was, in hysterics in her own kitchen because she couldn't bear the thought of finding somewhere else to live. The breaking point wasn't the loss of her husband, or the discovery of his secret life, but the bricks and mortar that surrounded her. Widowhood was far more complex and disturbing than she'd ever imagined.

Perhaps then she was the perfect fit for a criminal career of her own, of an entirely different kind. It was obvious she didn't have much of a heart. If she found the money, then she'd jolly well spend it herself.

Two days later, Elise was still of the same mind. She was busy working through yet more records she needed to change now that Gerald was dead when the doorbell rang.

Secretly pleased not to have her head in paperwork, Elise trotted to the front door and opened it. Lottie stood on her doorstep with an expectant smile and a posy of yellow and white flowers.

"Hello, Lottie," she said. "Please, do come in. Would you like some tea?"

"Yes, thank you, that would be lovely."

"The flowers are for you, by the way. From our garden," Lottie said as Elise switched on the kettle and opened the tea caddy. She had never been a believer in tea bags. Real tea tasted far nicer.

"Thank you so much," Elise said and began to search for a suitable vase. "They're beautiful."

They were too. Though small, the posy – it wasn't large enough to be a bouquet – packed a powerful punch of colour. Early narcissi interspersed with a flurry of snowdrops formed the perfect winter-to-spring combination. The scent of the narcissi made Elise smile.

"I love the scented ones," she said.

"Me too," said Lottie.

While the kettle boiled and the tea brewed, the two women chatted about the elements that make up sharing a neighbourhood: the state of the Surrey roads; the occasional town floods; the weather and if spring might come early this year. For Elise, it felt blessedly normal to have a conversation which didn't involve the police or criminal gangs. She'd almost begun to forget what an ordinary life might be like, and this unexpected reminder was more than welcome.

When they finally sat down in the living room, and Elise leaned forward to pour the tea, Lottie coughed. "Look, you probably get this all the time at the moment, but honestly if there's anything you want, we're just next door so all you have to do is ask. If you need any help, with DIY for instance, please just say."

Elise laughed. "Thank you, again. But actually, Gerald always used to ask me if he wanted anything fixed. I was much better at DIY than he was, though if anything goes wrong with the electrics, I'd be grateful for the help. My hair is difficult enough to control without the addition of electricity."

Lottie laughed at that, but looked momentarily concerned. As if Elise was in the habit of regularly wetting her fingers and putting them into electric sockets as she passed by. Perhaps this kind of behaviour was what the neighbours expected of new widows? Elise once again stifled a smile. She wasn't the kind of woman to throw herself, metaphorically or indeed literally, on her husband's funeral pyre. Just think of the mess such an act would create for those people left behind. Besides, Gerald would have been shocked if she'd ever even contemplated such a thing.

It wasn't what he'd married her for.

Was it? Now there was a question Elise had never asked herself before. A strange time for the issue to come up in her head indeed, with the scent of winter flowers filling the air and the easy presence of her neighbour demanding a conversational response.

Her timing had never been perfect however. "Thank you," she said again, aware of the need to sound normal, especially to the neighbours. "That's really kind of you. I'll bear it in mind."

The conversation turned to Elise's garden, visible through the living room patio doors. She'd not done much to it since Gerald's death though of course there wasn't much to do during winter. As it was, the police had given the vegetable patch a good going-over in their search for the elusive money, so perhaps she should get round to doing something about it. Later, when she could bear the thought. Still, Elise was proud of the evergreen shrubs, and the winter-flowering heather was an essential splash of colour in the gloom.

But, goodness, how very middle class of her to think in this way. No wonder Gerald had chosen a far more exciting way of life. Perhaps it wouldn't have surprised her if he'd had another woman as part of his secrets too. Would it? The thought made her gasp in the middle of a sip of tea and she found herself choking and Lottie patting her back with concern. Though she wasn't sure patting the back was ever a solution to a coughing fit. Surely it would make things worse?

Soon Elise recovered, and was happy enough to listen to her neighbour. It appeared she admired Elise for her neat garden, even though this was the last type of garden Elise believed she had. During the summer, she was always on the look-out for stray weeds and the ubiquitous ground-elder. Really it was a constant war with nature, a state of affairs as far removed from order as Elise could imagine.

She was in fact so busy thinking about the secret life of gardens, orderly or not, that she missed the sudden silence in Lottie's conversation, and the feeling that it was up to herself to fill it.

"I'm sorry?" she said with an apologetic smile. "Could you say that again?"

Lottie accepted her apology with an expansive wave of her hand, which only just missed the teapot. Not that it would have mattered. There were no carpets downstairs as Gerald had always preferred wood. Did Elise? She wasn't sure. Something else to think about now her husband was gone. In the meantime, Lottie repeated her question, and Elise forced herself, firstly not to lose concentration and then, secondly, not to laugh. She did rather well at both, though she thought it herself and shouldn't.

"There are a lot of activities going on in the village," Lottie told her. "I know you and Gerald were never keen on joining much, but I didn't want you not to have the chance if you felt it was the right thing to do. For you, I mean. I know it's probably too soon, but if you wanted sometime in the future to join the book club, or the drama group, then you only have to ask. There's also the village tennis club, and I mustn't forget the croquet club. Though they're very serious and once you have a mallet in your hands, they never let you go. Anyway, I just thought I'd mention it, if that's all right."

For a few deeply horrific moments, Elise could see her widowed life in the village stretching out in front of her like a particularly intense scene from *The Archers*: reading books she'd never choose herself, being the prompt for the latest village play, and spending terribly posh lunch hours doing sports she had no talent for.

Was that all that was left for her? An ordinary life, the sort she'd been sentimentalising only a few moments ago?

If this was the case, then God help her indeed.

"Thank you," she said, pushing down the hysterical laughter threatening her calmness. "I'll certainly bear it in mind. It's very kind of you."

Elise worried for a moment that Lottie might press her to join one of these terrifying group activities right now, and she wouldn't be able to hide behind her promise to think about it. But perhaps pressing recent widows for commitment of some kind wasn't in the neighbourly etiquette handbook as the conversation moved on.

Half an hour or so later, and Lottie was saying goodbye, and inviting Elise round for tea at her house any time she liked. She seemed as if she meant it too, and Elise couldn't help but be touched by such openness. She wasn't a very social woman herself, not by any scale. She'd tried to be so when younger, but it had never succeeded. All in all, she preferred her own company. It was nice to be alone.

It was part of the reason why Gerald and she, in spite of their differences, had been so well suited. Neither of them had been people who liked socialising, and Elise could count on the fingers of half a hand, perhaps fewer, the number of times they'd had anyone round for dinner. Their house had always been their own, which was why entertaining Lottie with tea and conversation had seemed so very unlikely on so very many levels.

Elise had never comprehended why some people enjoyed the company of others. For herself, even though her job could be classed as a sociable one, she found contact with people meant that parts of herself were broken off as the day went on, and the level of sociability rose. Yes, this might be an overly dramatic image for a sensible woman, but it felt as true an image as she could express. By the end of the day, or the end of the conversation, Elise more often than not needed to withdraw into herself to build up her reserves again.

Gerald had been the same. He had been happiest on his own, and their best times had been spent sitting quietly in the living room, each involved in their own tasks. Alone, together. Well, she was certainly alone now, but no longer together with anyone.

Though, on second thoughts, Gerald hadn't been quite as alone as she'd thought, had he? If Elise had been the kind of woman who harrumphed, then now was the perfect moment for such a sound. But she wasn't, so she made do with stomping back to the kitchen and slamming the tea-tray down onto the nearest work surface. Not enough to break anything precious, but enough so the kitchen at least understood her feelings.

It seemed important.

If only she'd known about Gerald's secret life while he was still with them. Then again, what good would it have done? Elise didn't know how to respond correctly to the news her husband had been a recognised, if unconvicted criminal. Would it have been any better if he was alive?

She couldn't tell. For several minutes, Elise struggled to imagine a conversation when she confronted Gerald with evidence of his criminal activities. She closed her eyes and concentrated hard to help her get a better understanding of such a highly unlikely event, but it didn't help at all. She simply couldn't picture it. Gerald – towards her at least – had always been quietly-spoken, courteous and the last man she could ever imagine having been involved in anything illegal. Even now she could more easily put several of her colleagues into the role of criminal mastermind, more than she could her husband.

Perhaps she was in denial of some kind? Denial wasn't a state of mind Elise had much time for, so she was probably starting later than the average woman. Whatever the average woman might be.

It was time to stop churning everything round in her head and make some real decisions. How she hated indecision in anyone, and particularly in a woman. She would have a small gin to steady the ship, as it were – a phrase her grandmother was fond of using though to Elise's knowledge she'd never been at sea her whole life. Surely she deserved it and – again as her grandmother would have said – the sun must be over the yardarm somewhere in the empire.

It was six o'clock. Definitely the cocktail hour. Elise therefore put to one side all thoughts of arranging her widow's finances tonight, mainly by dint of finding Gerald's secret hideout, and made her way swiftly to her drinks cabinet. Or more accurately Gerald's drinks cabinet, until very recently.

She chose the London Gin, the one she'd always preferred, and added a good dose of tonic before returning to the kitchen for ice and the essential twist of lemon. *One of our five a day*, Gerald had always teased her and, to her own horror, she found herself tearing up at the memory of his words and the gently ironic way he'd said them.

Ridiculous! Such a silly thing to cry about. Welcome, she supposed, to the wonderful world of mourning. Grief was another kind of country and so far she wasn't enjoying the visit much.

She marched – and yes, that was the word for it – to the living room, sat down and enjoyed the first few essential sips of her gin.

Elise drank her gin and tonic slowly. She wasn't a daily drinker but three times a week she liked to sit down for fifteen minutes and ponder the magic of gin. Today was the first time she'd allowed herself to do so since Gerald's death. She wondered if this was progress.

While she waited for an answer to that particular knotty problem, Elise sipped her drink and gazed out at the garden. She wasn't really seeing it though. She was thinking about today and yesterday, and what it might mean for tomorrow.

Because it seemed to Elise right here and right now that she had two choices, neither of which was perfect, although she had definite views on both. Lottie, and also her office, represented the normal kind of a life she was supposed to lead now: husband-free (though absolutely not by choice) and with her days full of activities favoured by middle-class, middle-aged women across England. Good works, charity and eventual death. The thought of this made her stomach feel in need of a lot more gin than she currently had in the house, so she took a larger sip instead to steady her nerves.

On the other hand, there was another kind of a choice, and not one she'd ever considered before. Finding the money, hiding it from the police and Luke, and enjoying herself by doing exactly what she damn well wanted to.

Could she really put her brain to the test and find Gerald's ill-gotten gains when the police and Luke's gang could not? More than that, could she cope with the concept of danger and walking, however lightly, on the wrong side of the law? Ridiculous – of course she could! Perhaps it was high time in her life to allow herself the opportunity to live a little, and to give those wretched police something else to worry about – now poor Gerald was no longer their concern.

The memory of her encounter with the police brought Elise near to harrumphing point once more, and she had to resort to refreshing her gin – a most unusual occurrence as she normally allocated herself just the one. It was this perhaps more than anything else which led her slowly but with a growing excitement down the path of wondering what being a criminal and living – consciously – on criminal proceedings might be like. Anything indeed was better than the thought of being a middle-class and no doubt invisible woman.

She didn't have any desire to be an invisible woman and wasn't intending to start now. Neither was she the kind of woman to enter a new venture without any information whatsoever. She therefore needed to know more. The best way to get what she needed was never the most obvious one, however. Over fifty years on the planet had taught her that. It has also taught her that if you wanted to find anything out, it was best to ask the womenfolk and leave the men alone.

Elise finished her gin and tonic. Then she picked up the phone and dialled the number Luke had kindly given her.

"Good afternoon, Luke," Elise said, when he answered. "If I may, I'd like to talk with Janet."

## Chapter Twelve

Elise met Janet in one of the European style cafes in Godalming. It had taken several more telephone calls to persuade her to chat, and Elise wondered if it was simply because Janet wasn't the chatting kind – in which case she herself had every sympathy – or if there was something more going on – in which case she most definitely needed to know. The truth was very important to her, especially when it concerned missing money.

Not that the truth had mattered for Gerald, had it? He lived a lie all those years in their marriage, and Elise had never had a notion anything might be wrong. Yes, they weren't the easiest of married couples, but what they had worked for them, or so she had thought. Now, she wasn't so sure.

Janet had been quiet when she arrived, even though her stature had caused several stares from other customers as she walked across to Elise, who as was her wont had arrived early. She had always believed early arrival gave her an advantage and time to prepare but, looking at Janet, she wasn't convinced preparation would do any good. She would have to go with her instinct. She hoped it might be enough.

By the time Janet reached her, all those staring had been forced to look away as she swept them with a swift cold glare. Elise hoped there wouldn't be trouble. She'd never much warmed to trouble. Then again, perhaps it was time to learn.

"What can I get you?" she asked as Janet manoeuvred her considerable bulk into the chair. "My treat."

If Elise had expected something robust and powerful in coffee terms, she was proved wrong.

Her companion's expression lightened. "Thanks. I'd love a decaff skinny latte with a sprinkle of cinnamon, and a blueberry muffin. But only if you're eating too, and on one condition."

"What's that?" Elise enquired, already halfway out of her chair and reaching for her purse.

"You can never tell anyone else what I ordered. When I'm with the lads, I go for Americano, full-fat with one sugar. I hate it but it means they don't question my abilities. And I don't like people questioning my abilities."

Elise laughed. "Me neither. I resent it. If it should happen, I make sure it doesn't happen again. That said, I can't imagine anyone foolish enough to try to question you, Janet. You exude ability."

With that, Elise stepped off smartly to put in her drinks order. She was sure, as she left the table, that Janet was blushing. This too made her smile.

A few minutes later and Elise was back at the table, with Janet's order on a tray alongside her own black coffee and plain flapjack. She always thought it rude to let people eat on their own. Besides she could do with the nourishment.

Never one for small talk, however, Elise allowed Janet only one bite of the muffin and three swallows of coffee before she skipped straight to the main point.

"The thing is, Janet," Elise began, "Luke thinks I have the ability to find where Gerald hid the money he stole."

She took a breath to carry on but a large and capable hand across her mouth brought a sudden halt to her words.

"Hush," Janet said. "We don't like anyone using the word 'stole' in relation to our business activities. You never know who might be listening and they could well get the wrong idea."

"But nobody's listening. And, besides, I'm keeping my voice down," Elise protested.

Janet shook her head. "It's worse when you whisper. The moment whispering starts, everyone shuts up, stops what they were doing and tries to focus on what the whisperer is saying. It's a known fact."

"Really?" Elise suddenly became conscious she was whispering and glanced round quickly to see what effect it was having on their fellow coffee-drinkers. She suspected it would be nothing, but she suspected wrongly. As she swung round, tracking the few groups of people in the café, she could see two young lads staring at her and one or two sets of others making an impressive effort not to glance her way. Still, something in the way they were sitting told her she'd been drawing attention to herself by trying not to do so.

She couldn't help it. She began to laugh. "You mean the way to stop people from listening to your business details is to shout it from the rooftops?"

"Oh yes," Janet replied, her face deadpan. "Listen."

She drew up her considerable bulk, coughed and spoke in the sort of voice that carried the whole of the coffee shop and no doubt into a large section of the High Street outside. "My companion and I are planning a murder," she said. "We thought of poison as a means, but it's too dull. Really, everyone needs more blood, so a knife is our weapon of choice. The only trouble is we've not decided upon the victim yet. Any offers?"

The catering staff sniggered from their safe haven behind the bar, but subsided when Janet flashed them a look. The sort of look that might well have stopped the rush hour traffic on the A3. Elise wished she had that kind of talent. She would be sure to practise her facial expressions in front of the mirror tonight.

Elsewhere in the café, people shook themselves, turned away and continued to chat about whatever the topic of the moment had been before Elise began whispering.

Elise blinked as the focus of attention drifted inexorably away from Janet and herself. "Goodness, you might be right. Little wonder you're such a successful business."

Janet shrugged nonchalantly. "Thank you. Though I have to say your husband had a lot to do with it, Mrs. Walker. He was a great inspiration, and Luke will do his very best to live up to the example he set. We'd like to do Mr. Walker proud, wherever he is now."

Elise nodded her thanks. She wasn't convinced Gerald remained anywhere within earshot, but she could appreciate Janet's courtesy. Once one was dead, one was dead and there was no coming back, in any guise.

"Anyway," Janet continued. "That's as may be, as my aunt always says. It's not why you asked me here, is it? I know you don't do small talk and neither do I. So what's on your mind, Mrs Walker? I'll try to help if I can, though my loyalties lie elsewhere, I have to tell you."

Elise had no problem understanding. Her loyalties lay elsewhere also, but she was after information, so she came straight to the point. "Luke, and indeed the police, say Gerald stole money and hid it somewhere. It's not in the house, or the garden, as they've looked and found nothing. I don't know where it is, and it's obvious Luke doesn't know either or he wouldn't have asked me. Now Gerald – at least with me – was a man of very strict routines in his daily life. In the domestic arena, I don't think there's anything I don't know about him. Or at least that was what I thought I knew."

Janet shook her head gently, and Elise saw a smidgeon of compassion in her gaze. "He kept his two lives very separate," the bodyguard said quietly. "We always knew it. I'm only sorry he wouldn't allow himself to let you know it too. Mr. Walker always imagined you'd think less of him if you knew, but I think he was wrong. It wouldn't have made any difference at all to you, would it, Mrs. Walker?"

Elise blinked. "No, it wouldn't have made any difference," she said. "I do wish Gerald could have known it. I wish he could have trusted me."

She wanted to say more but, unexpectedly, she couldn't. Her eyes filled with tears. Janet pushed a tissue into her hand, and Elise used it. "I'm sorry. I don't mean to be ridiculous."

"You're not being ridiculous. These things are difficult. Even more difficult now you've discovered Gerald's secret life. Not that there was anything dodgy about it – not as far as we see it anyway. He didn't have another woman or anything like that. Which would be a lot worse, wouldn't it?"

Yes, Elise had to acknowledge. It would have. She was beyond glad she'd not had to raise the subject with Janet herself though and her curiosity had so easily been assuaged. Something about her companion told Elise she wasn't lying. So she could rest assured there had been no lurking mistress, and the only matter for concern was the money. She felt a wave of gratitude overpower her and, for that reason and that reason alone, she reached into her handbag and took out the paper with Gerald's cryptic message.

She laid it on the table before Janet's eyes. "There. It's the only odd thing I've found. Is it something you might recognise?"

"Allotment?" Janet shook her head. "No, it doesn't mean anything to me. Do you think Mr. Walker might have hidden the money on an allotment somewhere? Do you have any nearby? I couldn't tell you as I'm not a keen gardener."

Elise was more of a fair-weather gardener herself. "There aren't any in the village. The nearest is here in Godalming, but Gerald never visited as far as I know. Though obviously I don't know very much."

She was intending to say more, but Janet stopped her with a huge hand on her arm. "But, Mrs. Walker, you know far more than you think. Every man keeps secrets, don't they? They can be big ones or small ones, but they're still secrets. Men don't talk like women do. The boss's secret wasn't another woman or anything horrible like that. He always loved and admired you. It was obvious. The only thing he didn't tell you was his association with us, and most of our activities are carried out online. His day to day life was always with you, and that's really what counts. So if you say Gerald didn't visit the local allotments, then he didn't visit them."

Elise stared at Janet for a few seconds, and then found her face was wet once more. She didn't reply. There was no need. Since Gerald's death, she'd been haunted by thoughts of his secret life and had hated and loved him in equal measure. Now, Janet's simple words spoke to her in a place inside she'd left alone. A place she should have visited before now.  She and Gerald had been good together. Not perfect, but good. They'd suited each other, and they'd been a team. This, to her and also to him, had been more important than anything.

"You're right," Elise said at last in response to Janet's quiet concern. "Thank you for letting me remember it."

Janet smiled and released Elise's arm. She handed Gerald's note back to Elise. "No problem. I'd forget about this if I were you. Perhaps Mr. Walker was hoping to buy an allotment in the future? I doubt it means anything."

Yes, Elise thought Janet was probably right. She was being ridiculous and she should forget all about it and simply get on with her life. The other option was to search through all the allotments in the area secretly until she found the money Gerald was supposed to have hidden. Not a good plan for a middle-aged woman and she had no desire to have to deal with the police again, at any level. Besides perhaps Gerald hadn't hidden the money at all.

Perhaps it had simply gone missing. The Internet was a curious place.

Still, even as she said a polite goodbye to Janet and made her way home, Elise was thinking about the possibilities. She wasn't an expert in letting things go. She never had been.

So, at home, instead of disposing of the note, as Janet had suggested, Elise looked at it one more time. *Allotment*. What on earth could it mean? She pursed her lips and put the note back in her handbag.

Strictly speaking, she didn't need to think about it any more and she should get on with her life. But she would keep her options open. There was an approach she could admire.

## Chapter Thirteen

Meanwhile, there was work to cope with. Elise began to understand she'd reached the beginning of the end – or perhaps the end of the beginning – on the day of the departmental awayday. Initially she'd been commanded from on high to organise this illustrious event by the Registrar himself. The Registrar was a man who barely spoke a word to anyone and relied entirely on his very efficient, kindly and gently glamorous PA, Juliette, to be his link with the outside world. He'd never actually said anything to Elise, even though she was a member of his office and Hugh was the Deputy Registrar. Sometimes she wondered if he was aware of her presence at all.

All the more astonishing then that he'd asked her to organise the away event. Well, he'd not actually spoken to her himself. He'd asked Juliette to convey the terrible news. Elise was instinctively unable to refuse Juliette anything, because she was such a lovely woman and so very helpful. Two things that Elise was distinctly not, so she always admired women who were. So for two weeks,

Elise had been in charge of finding a suitable date, in the current millennium, for all 250 staff across the division to get together for a morning of presentations, team building and fun. Which was how the Registrar apparently described the event.

While the unfortunate Juliette was relating this piece of managerial terror, Elise had to concentrate very hard on the image of poor Gerald's body on their hallway floor. This helped her not to burst into hysterical wails and run from the building. Fun was not part of Elise's repertoire and, in all her years of administrative effort, Elise had never once been to an away day where anything resembling fun ever took place. In her mind, it was corporate bullying writ large, and even more so if some well-meaning but misinformed manager took it into his – for it was never a *her* – head to make everyone do team building games. This was very definitely a male activity, though Gerald had always thought such events to be the work of the devil. This was the only time Elise had ever heard him speak in theological terms, and she couldn't help but agree.

So, for two whole weeks, until the Registrar realised it was not wise use of time to make a part-time staff member who did not actually work for him arrange a very important event, Elise attempted to do battle with the vagaries of the local sports park. This was the only venue in the area large enough to cater for 250 people (most of whom, she imagined, would actually flee to the hills if invited to a department-wide event) and which the university could afford. However, getting anyone to answer the phone or respond to any of her emails was an almost impossible task.

Finally, however, Elise managed to make contact with the other side and even make an appointment to see someone in charge of room bookings. For this very important date, she took Juliette with her on the grounds she didn't really have the first idea how to go about booking such a large event, and so it was wiser to take an expert.

This turned out to be a very good decision. Not least because although the sports park was the town's pride and joy, and had been in the local news more often than Penelope Keith, Elise didn't know how to get there. She and Gerald had always made it a point of honour never to go within two miles of any sporting facilities in case they became tainted by sweat and enthusiasm. She'd seen no reason to change her approach to exercise after his death – until, unfortunately, today.

Thankfully, Juliette – who, in any case, knew everything but in such a kind way that nobody minded – of course knew the way, so Elise followed her directions until they came to the vast emporium of sport.

Once inside, Elise was at a loss. The caverns of the reception area seemed to swallow her up so she wasn't sure if she'd ever be free of them. Still, the very thought of exercise had always had the same effect on her, so being this close to it was bound to feel wrong. Everyone looked so impossibly healthy. Heavens, she'd only been here for a moment and already she could see young people jogging along the corridor, chatting about some sporting event or other. She had no desperate wish to know anything more about it, and never would.

Not only that, but the sound of small balls being slammed into the wall echoed from all directions. How could the reception staff stand it? Elise liked to work in an atmosphere of peace and silence, and here she found the complete antithesis to her working practices. When she glanced over at reception, all three slim blonde twenty-year olds were smiling brightly and dressed as if about to attend their own sporting event.

Perhaps it was the company rule. Not one Elise was particularly partial to.

"Are you all right?" Juliette's gentle enquiry was accompanied by a concerned hand on her shoulder. Elise shook off her shocked frown, and found a smile instead. "Yes, I'm fine. This is my first visit here, that's all."

Juliette raised her eyebrows and Elise wondered if she'd failed some kind of secret secretarial test. She hoped so. She wasn't a great believer in tests. Then her companion smiled. "You'd better keep close to me then. It's easy to get lost in here."

This turned out to be true. Even though the sports centre was only recently opened, it quickly became obvious – at least to Elise – that the floor plan and room numbering system had been designed by an idiot. The corridors looped and wound around each other, and the room numbering leapt from 1 to 35 and back again to 16 as they walked by. She could see neither rhyme nor reason to it as she hurried along in Juliette's path. The only common factor was the sound of distant racquet games, shouting and the occasional splash. At least the pool was impressive, but it only reminded Elise of her terrifying school swimming lessons, so she was happy to hurry on.

Juliette's venue contact was a slight man who styled himself the Events Manager and showed them round three possible venues, all of which to Elise's untrained eye looked the same.

She was evidently wrong about this. From nowhere, the ever pleasant Juliette produced an electronic tape measure and began questioning the Manager about size of tables, footfall (whatever that might be), catering, presentation equipment, the stage area facilities and the terrible doom that would befall everyone if the seats were tiered. Apparently, the Registrar disliked the usual raked lecture theatre style.

However, the sports venue could do tiered or same-level seating, which gave them one plus point on Juliette's list. Elise couldn't help being impressed. She'd never been so committed to anything in her life that she wanted to list it on a sheet and tick its success. Perhaps she wasn't a natural secretary after all.

When the department finally came to the agonies of the day itself, Elise hadn't changed her opinion concerning her own skills. However, it was only in the second session of the away day that she began to fear seriously for her sanity. The Student Employability Manager was presenting a too long session on, logically enough, student employability. What this had to do with their department was anyone's guess, but Elise knew her opinions on the matter would be unwelcome. She liked to think she was the Voice of Cynicism in a university world gone mad, but she understood managerial tolerance of her own humanity only went so far. Jim, the Manager in question, was in the middle of showing them that they were – in personality terms – all either elephants, dolphins, tigers or monkeys.

Elise hadn't been listening very much to any of this so had no idea what they related to, though personally she always thought of herself as a cat. Silky fur but sharp claws when the times demanded it. Halfway through his talk, Jim retrieved one of his props from the stage, which happened to be a large furry gorilla, and for some unaccountable reason stuck his hand up it in order to demonstrate what a monkey looked like.

Elise snorted out the sip of water she'd just taken, and had to turn it into a coughing fit to avoid uncomfortable fallout. Jim gave her a worried glance, and she waved her apologies.

Glancing round, she saw everyone else was concentrating hard on his efforts. She was the only one who really, truly, wanted to spring to her feet and leave, if only in search of her lost humanity.

Not the only one, however. From across the hall, she caught Hugh's glance and, just for a moment or two, he smiled and raised his eyes to the ceiling. He looked as if he too could do with some means of escape, and Elise only wished she could find it for him. The fact that they shared their opinions about the talk warmed her.

Even so, the time had come to consider her future very carefully indeed. God forbid she would ever retire from this place. There absolutely had to be more to life than this.

Could she afford not to work at all? Gerald's death had left her comfortably off, though not as much as if she'd been allowed to keep his more illicit earnings. The police had done their work thoroughly, sad to say. They'd investigated her house, her finances and her life so very carefully she thought she was probably very lucky indeed to be left with anything.

Elise, a smile still fixed to her face to fool anyone who might expect her to take an interest in the shenanigans of the away day, allowed her attention to focus for a few moments on what was going on around her.

Not much had changed, as far as she could tell. The speaker with the cuddly toy collection had left the stage, thank goodness. In his place was one of the student support managers giving them a ten-minute presentation about what his department was doing. As Elise was very well aware what his department was doing and the presentation behind him looked the same as the one from last year, she didn't pay him much attention either.

Really, what was the point of getting everyone together to talk about what they already knew? Information could perfectly well be sent out by email. They were going over old ground.

*Old ground ...*

Something in Elise's memory clicked into place and she frowned. Something about old ground and something to do with her husband. What was it? For a moment she thought she had it, but then trying too hard sent the memory skittering away and she'd lost it once more. Typical.

A sudden scraping of chairs brought her out of her puzzlement, and she realised the student support talk had finished, and the employability man was back. They were now apparently at the 'interactive' part of the morning, Lord help them all, and some kind of practical response would be required. Elise groaned inwardly. Interactive responses, like fun, weren't her strong point.

The day dragged on but, like all bad and good things, it eventually came to an end. The following day, safely back in the office, Elise tried to process the many emails which had landed in her inbox during her absence yesterday.

She was still pondering her future. Had everything become far more complicated since she'd been a widow? Perhaps Gerald had possessed some kind of magic which had managed to protect her from the worst excesses of educational administrative traumas. Or – more likely – she was feeling vulnerable enough for the constant stream of demands, some more meaningful than others, to irritate her more than usual.

On a normal day, Elise simply dealt first with the emails marked 'urgent' or with those staff who shouted the loudest or who had the most executive clout, and fitted in the rest where she could. This didn't take into account the odd phonecall requesting her help, the everyday demands of Hugh, or indeed any of the people who worked in his team.

It always surprised her how, merely by dint of having worked at the University for over ten years, everyone assumed she knew everything. In actual fact, Elise had learnt very early on that if you looked confident enough and wore an open smile, you could get away with an awful lot. From this approach to her working life, Elise had unexpectedly created a policy on stationery ordering, the principles of presentation equipment use and – her one great administrative moment – even succeeded in persuading her colleagues that organising their own train travel was by far the quickest way of getting where they needed to be.

In truth, it wasn't, but Elise didn't like booking train tickets and staring at timetables, and wasn't prepared to do it very much. She did everything else that landed, sometimes from parts of the university she'd not even heard of, on her desk, so she felt entitled to have some kind of payback. Train tickets was hers.

Until this moment and this day, however, she'd always enjoyed her job on the whole, and had even seen some kind of purpose in it, no matter how much the University tried to restructure any kind of meaning into a vacuum from which it could never recover. At heart, in the midst of the strategic imperatives, project planning and soul-destroying management speak which only served to dehumanise the workplace, it was all about the students. Elise could very much identify with that fact, although she was too old for any student to consider her opinion might matter. As a young student herself, many years ago, she'd not taken seriously the thoughts or wisdom of anyone over the age of thirty-nine and she was far beyond that now.

On a whim, Elise decided all these emails surely wouldn't add up to much and she wasn't entirely sure why she was looking at them. Surely she was wasting her time scrolling through.

She didn't like to admit it, but sometimes – oh yes – sometimes she thought back to the pre-computer days with a sense of frustrated longing. How she'd loved writing memos and getting up from her desk to talk to people. These days there was little excuse. Did it matter much if an email or several went missing? After what Else had been through over the last month or two, the importance of the world of university administration had rather lost its shine.

Nonetheless, the day passed in the way many days at work did: a flurry of activity which Elise suspected would prove to be of little import when everything was changed again in six months' time; then two meetings where the same aspects of university life were discussed but with slightly different sets of people; and finally – the bulk of her job these days – the constant need to change meetings in order to suit people's obviously action-packed schedules.

Why did the university have to hold so many meetings? It never resulted in anything more useful being done. Most advances in the world were not carried out by means of a committee, and 99% of the minutes she had to take could have been better handled with a quick email or chat.

After all, if poor Gerald – not so poor, however! – had run a criminal enterprise for so many years without the need for a process plan and a strategy, it surely couldn't be the best way to get things done.

However, the university insisted on doing things in this way. When, at 4pm that afternoon, Elise laid down her pen at the end of a two-hour long meeting which had meant virtually nothing to her, she'd had enough.

As her boss rose to go back to his desk, she touched his arm. "Could I have a word, Hugh, before your next appointment?"

He smiled, his mouth quirking at the edges before glancing at his watch. "Of course. I think I've got a few minutes before I need to be elsewhere."

"Perhaps in your office?" she countered. Here, in the Registry meeting room, Elise felt more exposed even though nobody could see in. She had something very particular she needed to say.

In his office, Hugh made space for her on one of the meeting chairs. He wasn't the tidiest of men and the days had long since departed when Elise had thought of trying to bring order to his creative chaos. She rather liked the disorganisation. It made a change from her previous boss, who'd been a stickler for tidiness and had always known exactly where everything was at all times.

Elise also enjoyed the feeling of power it sometimes gave her that Hugh relied so heavily on her ability to know where he might have last filed something. This, of course, made the task she'd set herself more difficult.

She didn't bother to make small talk.

"I don't think I can take this any more," she said, with a wave of her hand to summon up all the nightmarish shenanigans of the university she'd so faithfully served for all these years. "I'm going to have to leave."

Hugh's face turned incredibly pale and he blinked at her. "What do you mean? I'm sorry about the state of my office, Elise, and I know we've discussed it in the past, but I didn't quite realise …"

"No, no," she interrupted, not wishing him to go down quite such a personal route. "That's not what I mean. Your office is fine. No, what I mean is I'd like to give my notice in, as I don't believe I fit in any more."

This time, Hugh had nothing to say. He stared at her and sat down, very quickly indeed. In fact, rather more quickly than he might have been intending as the speed of her boss's downward trajectory sent a wash of papers scattering over his desk from the resultant breeze. He didn't appear to notice, and Elise didn't like to point it out. Not at such a moment of evident high drama.

Still, even with her virtual bag well and truly packed, she remained his PA for now, and Elise – if she knew anything at all - certainly knew her duty. "Can I get you anything?" she asked. "Coffee? Water?"

He shook his head and waved his hand at her, as the last of the displaced papers settled gently next to his computer. "No, that's fine. I just don't know what to say. You've always been such a backbone of the university. I can't imagine the office without you, to be honest. What's the reason behind your wanting to leave, if I may ask? Is it because of Gerald?"

Elise wasn't sure how to answer his question, because it was and it wasn't, at the same time. It had nothing to do with being a grieving widow, but a lot to do with Gerald's secret criminal life. Hard to put any of that into words, however, and Hugh was expecting an answer of some kind.

"It is and it isn't," she said in the end and truthfully, when silence was no longer an option. "The fact Gerald is dead means I have a certain freedom, though it hasn't happened in the way I would have preferred to enjoy it. I want to take time out to think about what I should do next, and I'm afraid if I wait to do so, I'll be here until I retire, or worse, until I die too. It's not been a bad job, Hugh, and you've been a good boss – the very best – but I don't want this to be the last thing in life I can put to my name."

Another silence, this time a smaller one, and Elise wondered if she'd been too direct. Hugh was a man who preferred a subtler approach.

"All right," he said in the end. "Though I'd advise you take some time to think about it. I wouldn't want you to regret anything later. Besides, don't they say newly widowed people shouldn't make any snap decisions about the future?"

"Ah," said Elise. "I don't know what it's like for anyone else. I only have my own experience to consider. Besides, sometimes the best decisions you ever make are the instant ones."

She could see in an instant he didn't believe her. She'd made her decision quickly, yes, but there was enough reason and long-held thought behind it to last a lifetime.

After this, she and Hugh chatted for about half an hour more, but he didn't say anything to cause her to reconsider. So that very afternoon, Elise wrote out her letter of resignation, giving one month's notice as specified in her job contract, and took the letter up to the HR department. She supposed she could just as well have sent it by email, but this seemed too important a moment to rely on a system where key moments were there and gone in an instant. Naturally, she'd taken her own copy. She liked to keep things orderly.

As she entered the HR department – which Elise still secretly referred to as Personnel – she was confronted with the usual problem she faced whenever she had dealings with HR. All departments across the university had their own HR representative and Elise knew the woman she needed to speak to was called Louise. She'd actually met Louise several times over the years and they possessed that uniquely courteous but distant friendship which was only ever found in the work place. However, for the life of her, Elise could never remember exactly which of the six young blonde women who worked in HR was Louise.

So she did what she usually did in these circumstances. She looked as confident as possible and, if all else failed, blamed her confusion on her reading glasses being back at her desk. There was something to be said for being the older woman – she could get away with rather more than she could when she was young.

"Louise?" she said with what she hoped was a merry smile, her glance taking in as many of the blonde women as possible, though not forgetting the one lone brown-haired young man.

That first terrible silence common in all open-plan offices when strangers appeared immediately followed, but

Elise was used to it by now. So she kept on smiling until, after what seemed like several hours but could only really have been a few moments, one of the young blonde women rose from her seat and trotted towards her, smiling just as broadly as Elise was.

She assumed this would be Louise, and indeed she vaguely recognised her so she hoped she was right. She took a deep breath and – goodness how very liberating it was – threw her customary caution to the four winds and far beyond.

"I'm here to give my notice in," she said.

## Chapter Fourteen

Having nothing at all to do was really rather diverting, Elise decided after the first week of not having to go to work. It was indeed the perfect time of year to give it all up.

In many ways she'd given up work at about the same time as giving up being a wife. She wondered who was typing Hugh's reports now. She would miss her quiet, but supportive boss. On her very last day, he'd hugged her as if he meant it and asked her to allow him to keep in touch. Though Elise had been surprised, she'd also been pleased, and had agreed with a swift flare of delight that had made her blink.

Before she'd departed, quietly and with no big party to endure, Elise had – as instructed – written out several dense pages of what the University termed as 'handover guidance' to the next post-holder. Every now and again, however, she'd thrown what could be called a 'wild card' into the mix so that instead of including a key part of whatever process she was describing, she left it out. And twice, she'd added in several administrative steps where they weren't necessary, just to see if anyone was paying her any attention now she was almost free of the working world.

It turned out they weren't. Because instead of having a quiet word or even shouting in astonishment across the office at her small rebellion once they'd read it through, Hugh and the Registrar had simply thanked her for her sterling efforts. It had almost made her laugh. It was astonishing what crimes a calm and confident smile and a straight gaze could allow one to get away with. Gerald, no doubt, would agree with her analysis.

However, she hoped the incoming post-holder, whoever she might be, might not be too disadvantaged by Elise's underhand cunning. She wasn't entirely without compassion.

Now, here she was, enjoying her new and relaxing life. It was early March, the bulbs were most definitely out and there was much in the garden and beyond to enjoy. So Elise set her mind to tending the earth around her. It was a very good feeling indeed. One of her first decisions was to remove Gerald's vegetable plot. She did feel a twinge of guilt but she had a future to consider, which didn't include home-grown vegetables. Yes, she'd enjoyed Gerald's offerings in the past, but to her it all seemed so much trouble for something you could buy perfectly easily at the village shop. She wasn't much of a one for *The Good Life*. And how that reference dated her.

Refusing to dwell on anything other than the matter in hand, Elise put on her oldest set of clothes – the ones she kept specifically for the garden – found her wellies and proceeded to dismantle Gerald's domain. It was far harder work than she had anticipated. The vegetable plot was made up of four raised beds framed by wood and surrounded by gravel. They had actually been here when Gerald and Elise had moved in and hadn't been part of their redesign of the garden.

However, dismantling the wood and lifting the soil would take some time and she wasn't sure if she had the energy today. Perhaps she'd start with something simpler.

So she paused and looked around to see if anything fitted the bill. Next to the outside door leading to the garage stood a corner trough and climbing frame for roses. They'd used it once, a long time ago, but it tended to fall over in high winds so Gerald had moved it and weighed it down with old soil and stones to keep it steady. The rose which had originally accompanied it had long since died and they'd not bothered replacing it. Still, the frame and its attached trough had remained and had in some way become part of the garden.

She'd start there. It would be a small stepping stone to the vegetable plot's complete overhaul. She hunkered down, gripped her trowel and began to remove the trough's contents. A few minutes later and her trowel came up against something solid in the corner. Elise cursed, but softly. A stone, she imagined. Experimentally, she gave the stone – or rather rock, from the feel of it – a cautious shove with the trowel and was rewarded by a dull clanging sound.

This, whatever it was, was no rock. She loosened the earth around it, which took a while but she was no longer a young woman. Then she crouched down and tried to feel the shape of whatever it was, but her efforts to pull it into the light gained no success. She levered herself up, knees creaking, and went in search of a proper garden kneeler. If she was going to have to wiggle whatever it was out with her bare hands, then she'd make sure she was comfortable while she did it.

Five minutes later, Elise finally worked the object free and pulled it out of its earthly burial place onto her lap. She blinked, then blinked again and brushed the dust and dirt off the top with her gardening glove. A small rectangular metal box met her gaze. It was fastened with a clasp but this was broken, damage either sustained in the past or by her attempts to dislodge it with the trowel.

Had Gerald put it there? He used to joke about how the climbing trough was full of old ground from the vegetable plot and was almost like having his own portable allotment.

Oh. Of course. *Allotment.* How could she have been so stupid not to see it before now? Still, she'd had a lot on her mind and couldn't be blamed. Something shifted in her head and the next moment Elise was pulling at the lid, eager to get to the bottom of the mystery. Where she'd expected a struggle, she found none. The lid shot open, and Elise found herself gazing at more bundles of notes than she'd ever seen before in her life.

Not the kind of note you sent to a friend either, if you had one. This was the kind of note commonly found in such quantities in a bank, and not in the middle of a rose trough. Still unsure if what she was seeing was true or if for the first time ever she was having a delusion, Elise pushed her hand deep in the box and brought out as many bundles of cash as she could hold.

Goodness but she'd never felt quite so powerful before. Money – the pure feel of it – was quite exhilarating. She would certainly have to revise her opinion of very rich people in the future.

A sudden wave of heat swept over her face at the thought that someone out there might be watching her. The police? Gerald's former gang members? Or, worse, the neighbours? The vegetable patch was overlooked, a factor that had slipped her mind.

She stuffed the notes back in the box, slammed the lid down and glanced up at the neighbour's window. The house wasn't Lottie's who lived one house beyond, but that of a man and his two sons who rarely spoke to anyone. They weren't rude, she thought, but simply shy. Elise gulped when a twitch of movement behind the shutters caught her eye. Had one of the teenage boys been watching? Goodness, it would be all over TwitFace by now, or whatever the young people were into these days. Elise didn't keep up with social media – she had never much wanted to share anything with her nearest and dearest; so why bother sharing it with strangers?

The world was a very peculiar place, to her way of thinking. However, without thinking about it one more moment, Elise jumped up, clutching the box and treading uncaringly across her kneeler, before trotting through the garage and into the house. She trailed mud behind her on her garden shoes, but the ground floors were wooden and right now she didn't much care.

She had far more important issues to consider. The first being how much money exactly was in this box and the second being whether there were any more of them. It took her a while to count it, especially as she was then sure she'd made a terrible mistake and counted it again. Then she counted it a third time. Better safe than sorry, and Elise always did like to be accurate.

Twenty thousand pounds. Good for Gerald! She should never have underestimated him before and she'd be certain never to do it again. Still, it wasn't the full amount, so what had he done with the rest?

Elise scampered – yes, that was the word for it, even for a middle-aged widow – back out to the now very desirable trough and dug through the rest of the soil. She checked very carefully to make sure nobody was looking this time and kept her back to the neighbour's window so they didn't see even if they did peer out. For all they knew, she was taking up Gerald's attempts to be self-sufficient, not driven by astonished greed. More fool them.

During the next half-hour, Elise found three more boxes, but couldn't find the fifth, no matter what she did. Maybe Gerald, bless him, had spent that one, though heaven knew it had definitely not been on clothes.

Anyway, the fact remained that she had four boxes, all of which appeared to be full to the brim with cash. A good job she'd not had a clue about any of the money while the police or the gang were asking the questions. Her innocence then had been real. Now it most definitely wouldn't be.

Currently her most important job was to check how much money she had. Funny how she was already claiming it as her own, even though it was more than obvious this was her husband's ill-gotten gains. Had he been saving it for them in some way? Perhaps he'd planned for the two of them to make a run for it and never be seen again? She hoped this was the case, and he hadn't planned to go on his own and leave her behind in a life of shame. Still, no matter now as she had it all – or almost all, Elise thought as she carefully counted up her unexpected contraband.

As before, when she reached the final figure, she counted it again and a third time. She liked to think of herself as a creature of routine, and today her routines were standing her in good stead. In total, she had eighty thousand pounds on her dining room table. It was a pleasing amount of money and she couldn't, for the life of her, work out what to do next. It would have been preferable if there'd been a fifth box, as the complete one hundred thousand pounds had a very satisfying ring to it, but Elise had never been a woman to reject what was on offer, especially if it was as good as this.

Could she put it in an ISA and save up for a very happy retirement? No, if Gerald hadn't been able to put it in a bank, then it must be dirty money and would probably be traced the moment she decided to spend it.

A good citizen would be ringing the police and handing it and all her spending problems over to the authorities. However, Elise had long since giving up being a good citizen. So, if she wasn't going to *do the decent thing*, as her mother would have put it, what were her options? Elise could only see one. She needed to get in touch with Gerald's old gang again, as there were one or two questions she needed answering

Elise decided to call Janet first. She answered at the second ring. "Mrs. Walker?"

Elise was impressed. "How did you know it was me?"

A snort came from the other end of the line. "You don't have caller display, do you?"

Elise had no idea what this might be so assumed the negative. "No, I don't. On the whole, I prefer to keep a sense of mystery about any callers for as long as possible."

This time the snort turned into an unmistakeable laugh. Elise swore she could probably have picked Janet's laughter out of a crowd of similarly aged amused women.

Her brand was very distinctive. Almost as distinctive, she hoped, as her own.

When Janet had finished laughing, Elise spoke again. "I've found what it was you and Luke were looking for. It's in the kitchen now. Or most of it anyway."

"How much?" Janet asked after a moment's silence.

"Eighty," Elise whispered, just in case anyone untoward was listening.

However, she wasn't a good phone whisperer, so Janet asked her to repeat it.

"Eighty," she said again, this time with more confidence.

"Eighty thousand pounds? Where did you find it?"

"I decided to move the climbing trough and frame, and there the boxes were, buried in the soil. The police obviously haven't done their job as well or as thoroughly as they told me they would. Four boxes in a neat row. Gerald was always a tidy man, but I don't know where the fifth one is."

"What are you going to do with it?" Janet chipped in.

"Well, I'm not going to the police, am I?" she answered. "I'm ringing you. I'm assuming the cash is marked in some way so the police will realise if we try and spend it. And I imagine you – as the gang who stole it – have some kind of system worked out, which explains my call."

A silence. Then Janet said, "No, it's not marked. And no, there's no system."

Elise blinked. "You mean we can spend it?"

"No," Janet said. "I mean *you* can spend it as I don't have it. Only you do."

Fair point and well made. Still, Elise had a further issue to raise. "You mean I can spend it without the police tracking my every move when I grow too rich too quickly, and then torturing me with truncheons to find my guilty secret?"

"I don't think this is Russia," Janet replied, her tone of voice deadpan perfection. "This is Surrey. But you have a point. The police are keeping a close eye on what we do now and you're included in that. Especially since our coffee in Godalming."

"Our coffee?" Elise queried. "What's that got to do with it?"

Janet sighed. "We weren't the only people having a drink that morning, were we? There were two plain-clothes policemen two tables down, though they weren't drinking much. Budgets must be shot to pieces."

"Oh," Elise replied. "Perhaps I do need some criminal support after all. I'm obviously an amateur. I think we should meet up. Where's the safest place?"

"Ah, that's easy," Janet said. "That'll be Winkworth Arboretum. Nothing exciting ever happens at a National Trust property so it's the best place to be when you want to be under the radar."

"Excellent," said Elise. "And the daffodils will be out. I'll meet you there in an hour."

She put the phone down and smiled. A potential life of ease beckoned her, but instinct told her without doubt that it wouldn't be as uncomplicated as she hoped. All the films and books she'd ever watched or read told her a life of crime – or living off criminal proceeds – was doomed to failure.

Was there another way of looking at it all? A way in which she could still benefit but wouldn't have to be glancing over her shoulder or jumping at shadows for the rest of her life?

Elise thought about it for a short while. Then she smiled again, but for a very different reason, and picked up the phone once more. She had a plan and she thought it a good one. The person she was calling might take some persuasion, but she believed in the end her suggestions would prevail.

Time would tell.

## Chapter Fifteen

Fifty minutes later, and Elise was sitting at one of the outside tables at Winkworth Arboretum, with a cup of coffee nestling at her elbow. She'd parked the car in one of the bays in the rough land car park near the café. It had taken her a couple of attempts as the bays were marked out by slats of wood, and Elise didn't always know where they might turn out to be during her parking efforts. It was ridiculous to use actual wood for parking. White lines were much better, as they didn't damage one's bumper when one made a mistake. One day she'd write to the National Trust and complain, but that day wasn't now, when there were far more important issues to consider.

Right now, she was waiting patiently for Janet and the gang – she assumed it wouldn't just be Janet – to arrive. In the meantime, she was imagining how she might spend the money and if she might have some left to put into a nice little pension. It was always wise to think of the future. Gerald always had, but not in the manner she'd previously thought.

If she had her way and, of course if she had a lot more money, she'd definitely buy an island somewhere warm but not hot. It would be about the size of the Isle of Wight and located right in the middle of the Mediterranean Sea. She'd always thought life was lived at a more humane pace on the continent. Here in England, and especially in the last ten years, she'd often felt as if she were doing nothing more productive than chasing her own tail. So, an island for certain. One with a large garden, with topiary. Elise was fond of topiary, though her patience could wear thin due to the slow growing nature of the box hedge. For this very reason, Gerald had never been keen.

This was daydreaming and she knew it. What would she really do with the money she had? No question about it, Elise would buy a library and fill it with all the books she'd loved over the years and would love one day soon when she met them. Everyone needed a library. Everyone needed to have something to read in the garden when the weeding was done. It was common sense.

"Elise? Is that you?"

A familiar voice startled her out of her reverie, and Elise looked up to see Hugh looming at her from behind the cake stand. His welcoming smile made her feel extraordinarily safe and also gave her an idea. A rather unexpected one. "Hugh! How lovely to see you. What brings you here?"

He waved his hand around vaguely as if about to introduce her to a group of friends he happened to be with whilst visiting Winkworth. The only problem with this possibility was that Hugh was standing alone with nobody else conveniently situated anywhere near him. Not even a passing old lady, and usually the National Trust was full of such persons.

Then again, Elise supposed in a few years' time she could very well fall under that category herself. Not yet, however. Not by a long way, oh no.

"Well, I …" Hugh began. He hesitated and then glanced round before taking a few steps closer to Elise's table. "Please, may I sit down?"

Any moment now, Janet and the gang could well arrive and revolutionise her financial life, but Elise was never one to refuse hospitality to a friend. "Of course," she said. "May I get you a drink?"

Hugh shook his head as his frame positioned itself, rather precariously, on the rickety seat. "No, I'm fine, thank you. But I'm really happy to see you as I need to explain something. It's important. You may not like it but I think it's time I came clean."

"Came clean? In what way?" Elise said, suddenly all too curious about what manner of sin Hugh might be about to confess. How very exciting life could be!

He blinked, then grasped the edge of the table with both hands as if it might fly off into the sky and never be seen again.

"It's this," he said, fixing her with a steady gaze. "I've liked you from the very beginning, Elise. Since the very first day you arrived in the office, I've liked you. You gave me a lecture on your first morning about the vital necessity of one good cup of coffee before any important decisions could ever be made. I've always remembered it, and over the years we've worked together, you've been proved right more times than I care to count. I also remember how at the end of your very first day you worked late, not because you needed to get urgent work out of the way or wanted to impress me, but because you couldn't remember how to get back to the car park and were waiting for me to be free to ask."

Oh yes, Elise could remember it very well. Well, the last part of Hugh's memories anyway. The coffee incident escaped her, though of course she was right. Coffee did make everything better and more manageable.

"I didn't want to disturb you, because you did look so busy," Elise said as Hugh paused.

He smiled. "It's an optical illusion. I'm never that much tied up with my work. But looking stressed helps keep senior management from the door just a little longer, which can make all the difference."

"To one's sanity."

"Absolutely." He agreed and then suddenly they were both laughing. Even as Elise kept an eye on the entrance the other side of the car park to make sure she knew when the gang arrived. This was the joy of Hugh. They could always find something to amuse them both.

"I love the fact we can laugh together," Hugh said, and Elise could only agree with him. Then he continued, "It's one of the things I treasure about you. In fact, and here's what I want to say to you so you'd better be ready – it's one of the reasons why I love you."

Elise stopped laughing, instantly, as if someone had snatched away all her merriment and replaced it with … with what, exactly? She wasn't sure entirely, but she did feel suddenly and surprisingly whole.

Goodness," she said. "That's nice."

"Nice? *Nice?* That's all you can say?" Hugh looked knocked back by her reaction, but in all honesty Elise hadn't meant it unkindly. It *was* nice, and she didn't care how English and restrained she sounded. She was English and restrained, so she had a perfect right to sound such. She was also thrilled with his words, but decided the best – the most truthful – reaction wouldn't and couldn't be conveyed in words at all.

So, without responding to his accusations of emotional numbness, Elise reached out, took hold of his collar, pulled him nearer herself and kissed him.

What a kiss it was. Oh yes indeed.

During the next few moments, however, Elise became aware of a low rumbling. Nothing to do with herself or Hugh, or indeed any of the good people innocently going about their business around them. But nonetheless it was a rumbling. A distant one at first but then growing ever louder and more insistent. She was about to question its presence even in the midst of their kiss when the world around them exploded.

A 4x4 hammered in through the Winkworth Arboretum gates. Or it would have done if the gates had been there. In fact, the souped-up jeep missed the gates entirely and drove straight through the wooden fencing into one of the three swings. Luckily it was empty. The children were all in school and their accompanying families elsewhere. The jeep didn't stop, and neither did the three other 4x4s behind it. All black, and all with blacked-out windows. They ploughed through the deserted play area and screeched to a halt in the mud between the trees. Only a few feet from where Elise and Hugh were sitting.

They both leapt to their feet. In the general melee and sound of confused shouts and screams, Elise was impressed at the sense of harmony between them. A good omen, she thought. At the same time, Luke, Janet and a bevy of other bodyguards sprang out of the crashed jeeps.

They were holding guns in a wide variety of sizes and colours. The gang had arrived then, and with rather more drama than Elise had anticipated. All her attempts to be subtle and criminally professional were shot – as it were – to pieces. She shouldn't have bothered, quite honestly.

Hugh reached out and grabbed her as if to protect her by his sheer proximity alone from any manner of guns and threats coming her way. Luke was at the table a mere heartbeat later, shadowed by Janet, Hank and Flank. She was heartened to note the guns weren't pointing at her, yet.

"Really, Janet," Elise said, determined to get the first word in, and happy to find her voice wasn't shaking. "I'd expected more of you than this."

Janet had the grace to blush, and Luke opened his mouth to speak. Before he could reply, two tables at the far end of the outdoor café were shoved to the ground and upended together to form a barrier. Several men jumped behind the tables and pointed yet more weaponry at them. Winkworth had never seen such drama, Elise was sure of it.

"Police!" yelled one of them. "Put your guns down and put your hands in the air, all of you!"

"We won't!" Luke yelled, and grabbed her away from her table, pulling her in front of him. Janet did the same to poor Hugh, and Elise wondered if he regretted his pursuit of her now.

She gave Luke a swift kick before he brought her fully under his control, and he cursed. It wasn't the act of a lady, but then again his act wasn't the act of a gentleman either, so the universe was probably more or less in balance. "Get off me! This isn't some Hollywood film," she protested.

From the corner of her eye, she could see Hugh struggling with Janet. Really, life after Gerald was proving to be rather astonishing.

"Put your guns down!" the ever-hopeful policeman yelled again.

At the same time, Janet let out a piercing and accusatory yell, and Elise twisted in Luke's grip to see that Hugh had somehow managed to bite her arm, and pull free from her clasp. Hugh? *Biting?* Really, things were looking up.

The momentary lapse in the law's attention as all heads swerved to take in the Janet and Hugh scenario gave

Elise her chance. She punched the unfortunate Luke in his groin. He yelped and let her go. Two pairs of guns from the two remaining free bodyguards turned instantly towards her. Hugh shouted a warning and this was when the police finally decided to stop negotiating and start fighting.

The policeman who'd shouted at Luke leapt bravely towards the men with the guns. Elise gave Luke a mighty shove, just as Hugh reached him and pulled him away from her.

What a hero.

"Come on!" she yelled at him. "We need to go. *Now*."

She expected hesitation but what she found in him was wholehearted enthusiasm. As the air behind them exploded into shouts, yells, screams and thumps – but thankfully no gunshots – Hugh grabbed Elise's hand and pulled her out of the fray and towards his car.

"Not your car! It has to be mine," she shouted.

Again, no hesitation. Hugh simply veered at an angle towards her little Fiesta.

"Have you got the key?" he yelled.

"Don't be stupid. It's not locked," Elise yelled back. "This is Surrey. We don't have crime."

"So I see," was Hugh's reply, and for once Elise had no response to him.

She reached the car. "Get in!"

Hugh scrambled round to the passenger door while Elise flung herself into the driver seat and fired up the ignition.

"Stop, police!" someone shouted at her. Presumably an actual policeman, though Elise didn't wait to find out. With Hugh only half in, she hit the accelerator and, with a roar of approval, her little car shot forward on its way to the exit.

Hugh landed with a bump and a muffled shout onto the passenger seat as she slammed the door shut. As Elise reached the exit amidst the general shouting and fracas behind her and swung the car to the right, away from Godalming, the three boxes that had been nestling on the seat fell to the carpet and broke open, revealing their contents.

"Good grief!" Hugh shouted, as they screeched round the corner and onto the wide open roads of Surrey. "That's money!"

"I know!"

"Goodness me." Hugh was silent for a while as they drove at high speed along the country lanes, though always taking due account of road safety. Elise didn't actually want to kill anyone. She stole a quick glance at him as she negotiated her planned getaway route through the Surrey countryside. He looked pale, perhaps even shell-shocked, but determined. She could admire that. "Are we on the run then?"

Good question. She owed it to him to be honest. "No, we're not. Not really, though the gang – Gerald's old criminal colleagues – do need to believe I've made a run for it. It's what the police and I decided earlier on, when I found the money Gerald stole. I did think, when I first discovered it, that it would be nice to have it all, so I arranged to meet up with the gang. Then I thought I ought to be cleverer. So I rang the police and made a deal with them instead."

"A deal?" Hugh sounded as if he wanted to say more but didn't know quite where to get the words.

"Yes. A deal," Elise continued as she kept on driving. "They need the arrests for their reports, so we've agreed I get to keep most of the money as long as I left one of the boxes with the gang when they came to meet me in order to incriminate them. It's under the table at the café. They've got twenty thousand pounds and I have sixty thousand. Job, as they say, done. By now, Luke and the gang have more worrying things to think about than whether I double-crossed them. In any case, I'm only the gangster's wife so, when it comes down to it, I'm small fry."

"No, Elise," Hugh answered. "You've never been that. You may be a gangster's wife, but you're the best gangster's wife I know. You're always full of surprises. What are you going to do with the money?"

"Why, thank you, Hugh," Elise said with a smile. "Stay for the ride and find out."

And that was exactly what he did.


THE END

Paperback edition
October 2015

## About Anne Brooke

Anne has been writing contemporary fiction and fantasy since Y2K. She is the bestselling author of thrillers *A Dangerous Man*, *Maloney's Law* and *The Bones of Summer,* all available at Amazon. Her websites can be found at www.annebrooke.com, www.gayreads.co.uk, www.gathandria.com and www.biblicalfiction.co.uk.

Anne's Amazon page: Author.to/AnneBrooke

Any questions or comments, please email: annebrooke1993@gmail.com

If you have enjoyed this book, please could you leave a brief review at Amazon by using the following link: http://myBook.to/GangstersWife. Reviews, however short, are a lifeline to independent authors such as myself, and I am very grateful for your time. Thank you!

Anne Brooke

18499371R00144

Printed in Poland
by Amazon Fulfillment
Poland Sp. z o.o., Wrocław